# THE WEALD OF YOUTH

also by Siegfried Sassoon

★

*Memoirs of a Fox-Hunting Man*

*Memoirs of an Infantry Officer*

*Sherston's Progress*

*The Old Century*

THE AUTHOR
*From a photograph taken in November, 1914*

# THE WEALD OF YOUTH

by

SIEGFRIED SASSOON

FABER AND FABER LIMITED
24 Russell Square
London

*First Published in October Mcmxlii*
*By Faber and Faber Limited*
24 *Russell Square London W.C.*1
*Second Impression Mcmxliii*
*Third Impression Mcmxliv*
*Printed in Great Britain by*
*Purnell and Sons Limited*
*Paulton, Somerset, and London*

*The paper and binding of this book*
*conform to authorized economy standards*

To

GLEN BYAM SHAW

*Looked on, the darkening weald grows dearer.*
*Weald of Youth, a remembered word.*

*S.S.*

# I

Late one afternoon, at the end of May, in the year 1909, I was driving myself home from Tunbridge Wells in our new dog-cart, which was a very comfortable one, two-wheeled, rubber-tyred, nicely varnished, and much the same colour as brown sherry. Under the seat was my cricket-bag. And beside me, below my straw hat, which I had placed over it for safety's sake, was this week's number of *The Academy*. To call it this week's number was an understatement of its significance; for it contained a sonnet to which my initials were reticently appended, and I was feeling appropriately elated. My sonnet wasn't an exhilarating one, for it was about the poet Villon when he was rather more down and out than usual. But there it was, for everybody to read; and when I got home I would read it again myself, with due appreciation of its finely-cadenced ending.

In the meantime I just glanced in its direction occasionally while the bay mare trotted placidly along the main road which we both knew so well. The setting sun was behind me. To the left of the high ground along which I was driving, the Weald lay in all its green contentedness. I was feeling fine, and had played quite a decent little innings in the match. But when I came to the cross-roads a mile and a half from home and caught that favourite glimpse of Kentish distance above the foreground apple orchards of King's Toll farm, the low-hilled blue horizon seemed alluring me toward my heart's desire, which was that I might some day be a really good poet.

My connection with *The Academy* dated from about two weeks before. Several London editors having sent back my sonnets with no comment except the usual printed regrets, I had tried *The Academy* as a last resort. I knew nothing of it except that it was advertised as ' liveliest of the literary weeklies ' and edited by a poet whose sonnets I had admired for their polished technical perfection. The prompt reply which I received is still in my possession, so I am able to transcribe it from the typewritten original—distinctive for its blurring purple-violet ink. ' Dear Sir, I have looked through the poems you were kind enough to send us, and I think that some of them might be used in *The Academy*. If you happen to be in town any morning next week you might perhaps call here and we could talk the matter over. Yours truly . . .'—for some time I couldn't be sure about the signature, which started with a series of what I can only describe as squiggles and concluded with a detached and dashingly problematic d. After studying it intently and sketchily by turns I decided that its illegibility could only mean T. W. H. Crosland. I didn't like this nearly as much as the rest of the letter. Crosland was remotely notorious to me as a powerful but repellently-pugilistic literary journalist; and although I was quite willing to talk the matter over with him on paper I felt averse to meeting him in the flesh, at his office or elsewhere. So I replied that I seldom came to London—which was true—but would be very glad for him to print some of my poems—which was also true. The immediate result was that he returned my poems with a brusquely impolite letter wherein he stated that as I couldn't come to see him he could have nothing more to do with them. Perturbed by this, I sent him a telegram expressing willingness to call on him on Tuesday or any other day that suited him.

Tuesday having received his ratification, I arrived at Lincoln's Inn Fields a little before the hour appointed. I had refrained from telling my mother the object of the expedition to town, merely saying that I had a new pair of riding-boots to try on and that I also intended to go to the Royal Academy. At that time Crosland's reputation as an author rested mainly on a vigorously provocative volume entitled *The Unspeakable Scot*. My mother had read it with exasperation. She was fond of Scotland; Robert Burns was one of her best-beloved writers; and Crosland, I had gathered, was 'unspeakably' rude to both of them!

Anyhow there I was, sprucely but soberly dressed, climbing the steep stairs to the unexpectedly poky office of the liveliest of the literary weeklies. Climbing also, I hoped, toward poetic reputation; for my batch of sonnets was in my pocket; and had they not already been approved by the sub-editorial eye? I had never before entered a newspaper office, so I not unnaturally regarded it as a turning-point in my career. Having blundered into a darkish anteroom (with one step down that needed knowing) I was informed, by an apathetic young woman who had emerged from beyond a dull-glazed door, that Mr. Crosland would be free in a few minutes. She then returned to her purple-violet typewriter, leaving me free to look at the review copies which were piled and littered about the room. Selecting one, which, I happen to remember, was a novel by Rafael Sabatini, I settled down to an inattentive perusal of cloak-and-dagger romance in the days of the Borgias. For about half-an-hour nothing else happened, except in Sabatini's novel and on the secretarial typewriter. Not that it mattered to me, for I had nothing to do before lunch except stroll about and restrain myself from spending money in second-hand bookshops. Meanwhile I wondered what Mr. Crosland was up to behind that other dull-glazed door with *Editorial* on it. Giving somebody beans in a slashing article, I assumed—no sound being audible except the occasional scroop of his chair as he pushed it back while searching his mind for a sufficiently rancorous epithet. Trenchant wasn't the word for it when Crosland got to work about the Women's Suffrage Movement, a pretentious minor poet, or the activities of almost all other literary editors, as I had discovered in my recent connings of *The Academy*. His personality, when I was at last allowed to sample it, proved to be very much what I'd expected. At any rate it seemed to have been so afterwards, when I was thinking him over and wondering how he could possibly have been different from what he was!

He greeted me abruptly and without geniality, half rising from his chair and pointing me to another one with a half-smoked cigar. A noticeable thing about him was that he had his hat on. It was one of those square high-crowned bowler hats which one associates with the judges at Cattle

Shows, and while he was talking it was tilted over his nose. Crosland was evidently a man who never wore his hat on the back of his head, possibly because he had long since lost all hope of wearing a halo. He had a dark heavy moustache, short side-whiskers, a strong harsh voice with a Lancashire accent, and a truculent blood-shot eye. Everything about him was truculent, in fact; even his nose looked antagonistic to the universe. Waiting for him to mention my poems, I listened, with startled shyness, to a half-humorous grumble about his difficulties in carrying on the paper. 'I'm always in a hobble about it,' he complained, adding that last time someone put up some money the editor planked it on a horse and lost the lot. This caused me to feel both impressed and perplexed by being told the stable secrets so early in our acquaintanceship. Perhaps he's mistaking me for a millionaire, I thought; but if he was hoping to persuade me to put up some more money he wasn't going about it with much adroitness! Shortly afterwards, however, he came to the point, praised my poems for their melodious refinement, and asked if I happened to have brought them with me. 'We'll give you a guinea each for them,' he remarked in an off-hand way when I had handed them over. A guinea each didn't sound very high pay; but there were nine of them, and to have had so many accepted 'all at one go' could only be regarded as a veritable triumph.

Apart from my verse contributions in boyhood to *Cricket, a Weekly Record of the Game*, I had made but one appearance in public print. This was a roundel called 'Dawn Dimness' which I had sent to a poetry magazine called *The Thrush*. That short-lived songster had paid me three and sixpence for it—the first money I had earned by my pen, or by anything else. So I was getting six times as much from *The Academy*, I thought, while I walked exultantly away from Lincoln's Inn Fields, never slackening my speed—except when I bumped into people and apologized—till I arrived at the quiet club in St. James's Street to which I had been elected about a year before. Yes, one could do quite a lot with nine guineas, I decided; and it never occurred to me that I should never be paid at all, which was what did happen (if not being paid can be counted as an event). Nor, apparently, did it occur to me that my reputation would not be greatly increased by the poems being signed with my initials only. I had already adopted this procedure in *The Thrush*, and Crosland had accepted my similar reservation without comment. This instinct for anonymity has been with me all my life. Success was, of course, my objective; but when it came to the point of them being printed, I somehow preferred my poems to be more successful than myself. It was also a bit embarrassing to think of my poetry being read by the non-literary people I knew. Not that the general run of those with whom I hunted and played cricket were likely to be even casual readers of *The Academy*. But if someone did happen to come across it, how would he respond to such lines as:

*Blind from the goblin-haunted glooms of night,*
*Passion with poisonous blossoms in her hair;*
*Then, crowned with rotted chaplets, wan Despair;*
*And Folly, from base deeds in headlong flight.*

How? . . . For that was how one of my *Academy* sonnets started off; and there was reason to believe that I should never hear the last of it if those lines caught the eye of certain members of the Blue Mantles Cricket Club. Already they were inclined to pull my leg, and it would never do for them to discover that I was what they would describe as 'a budding bard'. I cannot claim that these ideas actually entered my head while I was lunching sedately in St. James's Street; but they were somewhere in the offing—half-way between my boot-makers and the Royal Academy Exhibition, so to speak, these being the places where I occupied myself during the remainder of the afternoon.

* * *

Early in the spring of the previous year I had put forth my second privately-printed volume. This was a typically juvenile performance, though a shade more sophisticated than the naïve 1906 *Poems.* Entitled *Orpheus in Diloeryum*, it was in the form of an unactable one-act play which had never quite made up its mind whether to be satirical or serious. Sometimes I was pouring out my own imitative exuberances; sometimes I was parodying the preciosities of contemporary minor poetry; on one page I parodied Swinburne (crudely, but to me it sounded rather fine, all the same). Orpheus himself, by what I considered an effective dramatic device, made but one brief appearance, at the end, to admonish and stampede a clique of pseudo-artistic persons who had failed to recognize that he was the real thing, though disguised in a shepherd's cloak. Re-reading it now I don't altogether dislike it; there is something attractive about the unrevisable immaturities of one's youth. And Mr. Edmund Gosse—to whom I sent a copy at the suggestion of his friend my uncle Hamo—responded with a letter of lively encouragement. 'Your delicate and accomplished little masque,' he called it, adding that it reminded him of the strange entertainments of the early Renaissance, and of Italian humanism generally. What exactly *was* Italian humanism, I wondered, wishing that I knew him well enough to discuss the matter with him. As yet, however, I scarcely knew him by sight, though Mrs. Gosse had stayed with us several times. I had, in fact, seen him but once, and that had been long ago, when I was only about seventeen and far too shy to ask him anything at all; in addition to which the place where I had gazed upon him had been the Hampstead Town Hall—the occasion being a dance given by Mrs. Gosse and my aunt Mrs. Hamo Thornycroft. Mr. Gosse had looked a little agitated, I thought, as though he wasn't addicted to giving dances—or even going to them. All the young people were in fancy dress (what did I 'go as'? I wonder) and his professorial evening clothes and gleaming spectacles suggested that he would be more authentically 'at home' were he delivering a lecture on Congreve or someone like that. It wasn't a bit like the strange entertainments of the early Renaissance, but I thoroughly enjoyed myself. Meanwhile Mr. Gosse ended his letter by saying that he had observed, with great satisfaction, my richness of fancy and command of melodious verse, and hoped that I should make a prolonged study of the art of poetry and advance in it from height to height. I happen to remember that I received the letter while staying at Rye for a week's golf, and with such commendations in my pocket I could well afford to refrain for awhile from swearing at my wayward iron-play and the soaring wildness of my wooden club shots. My prospects of ever entering for the Amateur Championship were derisory; but Mr. Gosse was a champion among critics, and if he foresaw that I had a literary future, what mattered the loss of two brand new balls at the old dog-leg hole? (One in the dyke and one in the whins.)

More than twelve months after *Orpheus*, I was yet again employing The Athenaeum Press to print a thin volume. The rough proofs of *Sonnets and Verses* had already reached me when Crosland started sponsoring my poesy, but the piquancy of proof-reading was rather diluted by four of my pieces appearing in *The Academy* in five weeks. I began to feel that my initials were almost a public character! Then, after a fortnight's absence, I was again in the limelight with 'Passion with poisonous blossoms in her hair' and her symbolical associates. On that same day arrived the package containing copies of *Sonnets and Verses*—thirty-five in stiff white cartridge-paper covers and three on hand-made paper bound in black buckram. Resolved to do it in style this time, I had instructed the printer to use some red ink on the title-page. *Sonnets* was in bold scarlet type, and so was *Verses. And* (smaller) was in black, as was ' Printed for Private Circulation '. *1909* was red. Where my name might have been there was only a quotation from Pliny which I had culled from Montaigne's Essays. ' There is no such kinship between heaven and us that through our destiny the shining of the stars should be mortal as we are.' Printed in the original Latin, it supplied, I thought, a nice touch of scholarship, though I was no scholar, and many of the poems more than hinted that I differed from Pliny about heaven. There was also a bill for seven guineas, which was three pounds more than they had charged for *Orpheus in Diloeryum.* But I was already owed five guineas by *The Academy*, so I was more or less holding my own on the business side of poetry, though still obliged to economize as the result of having bought—toward the end of last hunting season—a glum iron-grey horse who wouldn't jump timber, had since become a confirmed crib-biter and wind-sucker, and was now being got rid of for a good deal less than I'd given for him.

In the meantime I was admiring the buckram copies by the yellow light of two candles on the writing desk in my lofty book-room out in the Studio. One was for my mother; one for myself. To whom should I present the third? Now at the beginning of the second part of the book—*Verses*—I had inserted a prose quotation from C. M. Doughty. Why not send him a hand-made paper copy, I thought, never doubting that he would at any rate read it all through. The phrase ' read it all through ', took me back to the day, nearly two years before, when I had discovered Doughty's enormous epic *The Dawn in Britain*, which, as everyone should know, is three times as long as *Paradise Lost*, pre-Miltonic in language, and comprehensive of about five centuries of ancient history. Made aware of its existence by a long and respectful review, I acquired the six green volumes and prepared to plough through the lot. This I did, though my attention wandered fairly frequently from the printed page. It was unlike anything I'd experienced in verse; and often, when I was becoming admittedly bored, I was rewarded by passages of enchantingly archaic beauty and poetic freshness. Realizing that this C. M. Doughty was an important writer, I took the liberty of congratulating him on his immense achievement, which—as my letter somewhat gauchely informed him—I had 'read all through'. I wanted him to know that fact, because it seemed to me that the number of people who had done so must be, for the present, small. At that time I was ignorant of the existence of his *Travels in Arabia Deserta*, little known then, but since acknowledged as a masterpiece of unique quality. So I took it upon myself to suspect that Doughty needed encouragement from the public, although I had an idea that most authors rather disliked receiving letters from total strangers. I did not anticipate that a reply would be forthcoming. As well might one expect any response to an epistle addressed to Mount Everest. Reply he did, though, and from no farther away than Eastbourne (which, by an odd coincidence, was where the dealer lived who had sold me my crib-biting grey). 'My dear Sir,' he began (had anyone ever addressed me as my dear sir before?) and continued as follows, with most charming courtesy . . . 'I am much obliged to you for your kind letter. I hope that the *Dawn in B.* may be and continue to be of service to the Patria. I remember when I returned from Arabia in '78, I had the pleasure of meeting some kindly there resident members of the Sassoon Family, at Poona (India). Your neighbour, Major Horrocks, is also a friend of mine. Believe me yours very faithfully, Ch. M. Doughty.'

'Well I'm blowed! Fancy Doughty knowing old Major Horrocks!' I exclaimed to myself, dismissing the '78 Poona-resident members of the family as hopelessly beyond my latter day cognizance. And a few weeks afterwards, happening to meet the Major in the road on my way home from a bad day with the West Kent hounds, I asked him if he remembered knowing an old chap called Doughty.

'Know him?' he replied. 'Of course I do! Lived in Tunbridge Wells till a few years ago and came here quite often. Used to buy his potatoes from me too. Great traveller, Doughty—knows the Near East as well as the palm of his hand!'

Jogging on up the hill, I marvelled at the smallness of a world wherein the author of the *Dawn in B.* had been putting the finishing touches to it within seven miles of our house and driving over to have luncheon with the Major at Mascalls. But when I had seen the frontispiece photograph of him in the abridged edition of *Arabia Deserta* (published about two months afterwards) I decided that Doughty was just the sort of delightful bearded old buffer one would expect to meet at Mascalls—the Major being a man who had somehow collected an admirable assortment of fine-flavoured cronies, aristocratic, unconventional, and connoisseurish. Over and above all that, the wonderful opening paragraph of the *Travels* took me by the arm and made me follow the narrator wherever he went on his immortal pilgrimage. 'A new voice hailed me of an old friend' . . . Those are his first words; and thuswise, in a sense, it happened with me. The epic poem had been a voice which sometimes sent my mind to sleep. To the Arabian traveller I listened with close attentiveness, accepting from the outset those quaint quixotries of style which are essential to his idiom. Here and there I found sentences of such memorable loveliness that I transcribed them in my manuscript book of favourite poems; and it was one of these that I had taken as the motto for my *Verses*. 'In the first evening hour there is some merrymake of drum-beating and soft fluting, and Arcadian sweetness of the Persians singing in the tents about us; in others they chant together some piece of their devotion.' The connexion between these words and my *Verses* will have been, I take it, that my supposed Persian ancestry qualified me to claim that I was singing in my tent, and that some of my pieces were devotional. (I may even have remembered my tent on the lawn during childhood recovery from an illness, when I sniffed the phial which had formerly contained attar of roses.)

Meanwhile I was still out in the Studio making up my mind to send Doughty a black buckram copy. This I proceeded to do, enclosing a short letter of homage to his *Arabia* and drawing attention to the quotation. Assuming that he perused this extract, Doughty must also have at any rate observed the presence of the little poem (in prelusive italics) on the opposite page, and for that reason I am reproducing it here.

*What shall the minstrel sing,*
*Touching his lute by the way,*
*Ye who are sad for the spring*
*Or for summer arrayed like a rose,*
*When evening comes to your day*
*And autumn draws to a close?*
*To them that are weary and gray,*
*Whose delight like life taketh wing,*
*Touching his lute by the way,*
*What shall the minstrel sing?*

Worse lyrics have probably been written at two-and-twenty. But the question—what exactly *should* I sing?—was one which I had not so far asked myself with any awareness of the circumstance that, like many minstrels of my age, I had nothing much to sing about. All the same, I choose to perceive in the pensive ditty some tenuous prediction of my present occupation as a stereoscopic memoirizer; because it is indeed for 'them that are weary and gray' that I am wearing out my eyes and elbows over these unlurid and localized reminiscences.

After which pardonable parenthesis I resume my industry at the stereoscope. Within a week I received a brief but urbane acknowledgement from Doughty (whom I was unable to think of as Mr.). From Kirkby Lonsdale he wrote that my book had reached him 'in this upland of fells and burns', and that he 'would now read it with interest and pleasure'. Whether he did so will never be known. Nor did he surmise that the word 'burns' had since acquired an associative significance in connexion with my book. For I must explain that his copy had narrowly escaped becoming unique! Was there a conflagration in the Studio? you speculate. Yes; there was; but it was a deliberately contrived one. After giving away one 'ordinary copy' I had destroyed all the others with the exception of the 'black buckrams', which I couldn't quite bring myself to put on the fire.

I cannot clearly recall the exact cause of this impulsive holocaust. Examining my work in perhaps too critical a mood, I had found a good many lines which obtrusively demanded revision, and several of the short poems had for the first time revealed their full feebleness. I had been polishing them for several months; but why, O why hadn't I waited a few months more?—I asked of the Studio skylight. For the impeccability of print and paper made my inadequacies only too apparent. ' Old days that are filled with the fragrance of dream ' . . . How ever had I overlooked the banality of a line like that? I began to suspect that even the Academy-accepted sonnets weren't as Parnassian as I had hitherto believed them to be.

I had already conferred a copy on our old friend Helen Wirgman, who happened to be paying us one of her long summer visits. ' Wirgie ', who hasn't appeared in these pages since some way back in ' The Old Century '—it will be remembered that we took temporary leave of her just as she had unfolded her parasol on the morning of Diamond Jubilee Day—Wirgie, I repeat, (the name being dear to my memory) uttered nothing, when next I met her, to suggest that my latest poems had disappointed her; but she did somehow imply, by her manner of commenting on them, that I should beyond all doubt do better next time. Anyhow I got myself into a tantrum about them, and without allowing my mother a glimpse of the volume went back to the Studio, lit a blazing fire—though the evening was warm and we had been sitting in the garden after dinner—and with self-martyring satisfaction fed the flames until my thirty-four copies, torn to hapless halves, were no more than a shuffle of smouldering ashes. When I confessed to Wirgie what I had done, she gave me one of her slow sad looks and remarked that I sometimes reminded her vividly of my Aunt Lula. And I remembered how Aunt Lula had, in that very Studio, long years ago, smashed her newly-finished bust with a hammer!

My own copy of the book survives as a sad reminder of seven guineas thrown away. What I did with the third one I am unable to remember. But I can assure the hypothetical owner that only its black buckram binding saved it!

## II

Some way back I have defined this book as an attempt to compose an outline of my mental history. That sounds safe and comfortable enough, and can be kept moderately plausible while the said history is unfolding itself through actual episodes such as were made use of in the preceding chapter. For it is seldom difficult to talk about one's own behaviour, mental or otherwise.

But when it comes to investigating the gradual development of the mind itself, then one can't avoid wondering whether any definable outline existed at all—especially in a mind so dreamy and undisciplined in its workings.

In addition it seems reasonable to ask how a mind which understood so little of itself at the time can be analysed and explained by its owner thirty years afterwards! The problem is indeed profoundly perplexing, and suggests much heavy work in store for the reader of the present chapter.

Let me therefore assure that reader of my intention to handle the matter as unfatiguingly as possible. All that appears to be needed is a simple chart of my mental climate in relation to a few of the writers by whom I was being influenced.

One must take for granted, of course, a fair amount of overlapping in my hasty and unsettled enthusiasms; but it can be assumed that by the beginning of 1908 I was no longer wholly swayed by the 'multiform circumfluence manifold' of Tennyson, Swinburne, and Rossetti, and that for the next couple of years I was exploring a medley of poetry, both good and inferior, in a desultory and unchartable manner.

The outcome of this, when surveyed in my own writings, was not altogether reassuring, as was demonstrated by the destruction of *Sonnets and Verses*. After that I resolved to resist the temptation to write in a loosely uplifting way on outdoor subjects, which was what I'd been in the habit of doing when feeling most 'inspired'. During the next twelve months, therefore, I aimed at refinement rather than vigour. Perfection, I felt, could only be achieved through a distillation of imagination which was strangely and exquisitely remote from everyday experience. The result was that pseudo-archaic preciosities invaded my vocabulary. Sunsets became like stained-glass windows, and the moon took to coming up in a mystification of Celtic twilight. Poetry was a dream world into which I escaped through an esoteric door in my mind.

When Wirgie was staying at Weirleigh in the

summer of 1910 I showed her a few of my latest productions in verse, and once again she hinted that I was moving in a wrong direction. Wouldn't it be better if I were to put some solid thought into my poems, and go in for more honest everyday words? Somehow she felt that I ought to be writing in a more *physical* way. And what had happened to my admiration for George Meredith?

She had come slowly up the Studio stairs with my manuscript in her hand, and I had seen by her face that she didn't quite know what to say about it. I had hoped that she would be more encouraging, for the sonnets had been written in a fine frenzy of aureate unreality, and I had copied them out again with gloating satisfaction. Anyhow I silently slipped the manuscript into a drawer of my writing table, and she went back to her long chair on the lawn without another word.

Her question about my admiration for Meredith made very little impression on me at the time; but I see now that she could hardly have said anything more significant. Before coming to that, however, I must explain that Meredith had been her hero long before I had so much as learnt to read; she had exalted him above all other living writers, and had known him personally. She had therefore been highly delighted when—about two years before—I began reading him, and even went so far as to buy the library edition of his complete works. Disregarding her warning against gobbling too much of him at once, I galloped through a great deal of his poetry, most of which I was unable to digest, though its sometimes undecipherable condensations provided a vicarious sense of intellectual importance. But I returned afterwards to his few lyrical masterpieces, and was very properly thrilled by their exultant energy and descriptive loveliness. The only thing I found to complain of in them was that they were written with a technical ingenuity altogether impossible to echo or imitate. The magnetism of Meredith also carried me through several of his earlier novels. These I contrived to enjoy in a perplexedly assiduous way—their characterization and exhibition of high comedy being beyond my immature and untrained intelligence.

When Wirgie asked me what I had got from my strenuous perusal of *The Ordeal of Richard Feverel*, *Evan Harrington*, *and Harry Richmond*, which were the ones I liked best, I probably spoke of them in a tone of evasive omniscience, for like many young people I wasn't fond of admitting that I had found anything difficult to understand. I can be certain however that I made no secret of having been strongly moved by the chapters describing first love between Richard and Lucy—a rapt generalization unsurpassed by anything of its kind which I have read since. But the ultimate beauty of that idyllic meeting ' above green-flashing plunges of a weir ' is not what I have been leading up to. My point is that by using the word *physical* Wirgie had given me the clue that I needed, though I was unconscious of it at the time. She meant, as I now see it, that the feeling I put into my poetry was derived from delight in word-music and not from observation and experience of what I wrote about. And she realized that the only thing I had genuinely absorbed from Meredith was his sensuous perception of nature—the way he felt and described what I now know to have been certain parts of Hampshire and Surrey. She saw that my verbal imagery was becoming exclusively literary, while the opportunity for writing poetry was waiting for me all the time, as it were, in that view across the Weald from our garden. The vaguely instinctive nature-worship which I had sometimes tried to put into words needed to be expressed in a definite form.

' What has become of your admiration for Meredith? ' she had inquired, and might well have added—' And what about the laurel wreath you sent him when he died? ' For my mother and I had sent a really noble wreath, made from the big bay tree at the top of the peony walk; and Wirgie, who had been at Meredith's funeral, wrote afterwards to tell me that it was the only one worthy of him. She was also very much up in arms against the Westminster Abbey authorities who had refused to allow him to be buried there. I have her letter still. After describing the portrait of him by G. F. Watts as 'a complete failure', she ends with a fine declaration that 'age could not alter his inexpressible charm of voice, manner, and look; he never disappointed one in any way'. Her question—as I said before—was left unanswered when she went down the Studio stairs on that blue summer morning in 1910. The reply, however, was silently manifesting itself behind the glass doors of my biggest book-case. A whole shelf was filled by the stylish sequence of Meredith's complete works—minus one volume of *The Egoist*, which my mother was re-reading with rich enjoyment of its epigrammatic humour. But on the shelf above stood the elegant *édition de luxe* of Walter Pater, by whom Meredith had been pervasively superseded in the capricious microcosm of my mind.

Meredith, of course, was a robustly inspiriting influence. He affirmed his faith in courage, gloried in physical activity, called humour the sword of common sense, and refused to be downhearted about the iron-featured facts of human existence.

For a while I had responded to his heroic attitude; he seemed to be the sort of man one ought to try and emulate. I had felt much the same about Browning. Meredith was the spirit of earth in autumn; he trod the hill-tops and shouted his jubilate to the north-west wind; clouds towered above him transfigured like Olympus, making evanescence permanent ' and life—the thing at heart—his endless own '.

Then came Pater, with his *Imaginary Portraits* and their atmosphere of life treated as an ' act of recollection ', subdued to the stately movement and lulling cadences of his style. The reclusive tendency in my nature found in him its cloister and its abbey-church. Here was the bowed head overhearing consolation in the long chantings of distant choirs; here the rich renunciation of folded hands and of feet whose final wayfaring was toward enhaloed altars: here, too, the receptive nose, whereon the customary and aromatic oblation of incense and thurible could produce an effect almost of vehemence.

Thus having visited the rose-windowed sanctuary of his discreet and splendid prose, I became such a devotee of Pater that for the time being I could read no-one else. His fastidious erudition I accepted in a superficial way. My essential interest was for the romantic and enigmatic elements in his studies of sensitive temperaments in the picturesque past. It was rather as if I were attending a service in some cathedral where one didn't quite know what would happen next. . . . That verger who had demurely conducted me to my pew, for instance—where had I seen him before? Not in the quiet streets of Barchester, surely, but rather in a Graeco-Roman sculptured relief; from the plastic rhythms of some marble *Bacchanalia* in a museum those now unaccessoried eyes, it seemed, had met with mine. In the faces of the cathedral clergy, also, I was to detect elusive resemblances to mediaeval or monkish types which suggested affinity not only with the historic past, but with a past that had afforded them curious and uncanonical experiences which might at any moment be paralleled. And the Bishop himself, who is even now mounting the pulpit steps to deliver his Trinity Sunday sermon (another big storm gathering, while the nave grows duskier every moment), can one feel certain that with the first peal of thunder he will not violently discard mitre and vestments, to stand revealed as the veritable incarnation of Dionysus or Apollo? . . . In other words, Pater's writings contained episodes and conceptions of pagan supernaturalism which appealed very potently to my imagination. And let me add that my clumsy imitations of his style are offered as a testimony of my continued enjoyment of almost everything he wrote.

Meanwhile the 'simple chart of my mental climate' has become a diffused adumbration rather than an outline. All we know so far is that by the middle of 1910 I was writing with more artificiality and less unpremeditated art than in the two or three years previous. Documentary evidence seems to be needed. But none is available for analysis except those poems which have survived through being privately printed, and a fortuitously-preserved 1907 note-book full of rough drafts and casual scribblings. Let us then examine the twenty-four sonnets dating from before 1910, with the object of finding out what I had been writing about. For the sonnet was the form in which (like so many people) I felt most comfortable, though I used it somewhat loosely, seldom adhering to the strict Italian model and often indulging in irregular schemes of rhyming.

It must be borne in mind that there were not many things about which I found it possible to feel poetical. In addition to this—as will already have become obvious—my contact with human affairs had been narrow and unenterprising. It is therefore no shock to discover that I had only two favourite subjects. Investigation reveals that the two things about which I wrote with most fullness of feeling were music and the early morning. In ten of the sonnets there are references to music and musical instruments, and the theme of daybreak recurs even oftener. For me, music was the handmaid of the muse, and all roads led toward sunrise. Sunset had to play second fiddle.

Searching the sonnets for evidences of mental autobiography, I interpret—from an occasional line or two—something written with seeming unawareness of its significance. But such disclosures are shadowy and inferential, for I was commendably reticent about my inmost feelings. In these pages from the book of youth what is most apparent to me is an utter ingenuousness. Meeting that sonneteer, in his somnambulance of unsophistication, I rediscover simplicities which move me—not deeply, but with a sort of selfless wonder. I am reminded of the magnanimously uncomprehending emotion which accompanied the putting of those words on paper—words that then seemed as though no-one else had ever used them before.

*With eager infinite hearts I see them stand*
*Listening in dimness to the heavenward lark . . .*

While in the act of composing those lines I probably thought I was saying my final word about life. And why not—when my own heart was so young, so eager, and so infinite? What need was there to worry any more about literary originality when one's whole being felt like some grand mysterious chord of music?

*The Lord of Death and Time is far. Can He behold*
*One heart that would make Life a lovelier thing than*
*Dream?*

There the voice of my vanished self is re-emergent from between the crumpled covers of that 1907 note-book which I mentioned just now. For a moment, the youngness of the helter-skelter handwriting makes my overhearing of it more alive than if it spoke from the unblurred permanence of print. Then the ensilenced years divide us. And I am left to make the only comment which occurs to me—a tag from some forgotten popular song which comes into my head uncalled-for. . . . ' 'E dunno where 'e are.' . . .

★ ★ ★

In summer I didn't often wake early. But when I did, and had the gumption to get up and see the sunrise, I was always glad of it afterwards. In fact a few such ' getting-ups ' have dwelt in my remembrance ever since.

To be aware of a glimmer of light at my open window; to hear a cock crowing from the farm beyond the wood—his shrill challenge faintly echoed by another one in the distance; to listen for the first thrush or blackbird out in the dewy dimness of the garden: and then to slip on some clothes and creep downstairs, while the grandfather clock in the front hall ticked indulgently toward striking four and the high window by the carved oak linen-cupboard showed a brightening east through leaded panes . . . thus to have stood on those life-known stairs with some ordinary day of youth ahead of me—what was there in it to remember long afterwards, when so much that was so much more interesting has become blurred oblivion? . . . The house, with its stair-creaking silences, its drowsing stuffiness, and the queerness of its reflections in mirrors and the glass of dark pictures—this was only a vacated residue of the night before. Soon the same happenings would be going on again and the half-light of ghostliness would be gone. I see myself standing there, in that earliest perception of familiar things made unfamiliar by the secrecy and strangeness of the hour, vaguely unsatisfied with the self whose expectancy had experienced so little beyond those walls, whose heart's journey had so long and so weary a way to go. The house was like an old person resigned to uneventfulness and nothing new, unmindful of my transient immaturity which was haunting it with heart-ache for freedom and fulfilment.

But out on the lawn the Eden freshness was like something never breathed before. In a purified ecstasy I inhaled the smell of dew-soaked grass, and all the goodness of being alive now met me in a moment, as I stood on the door-step outside the drawing-room. In the eastward windows of the Studio the cloud shoals of daybreak were beginning to be reflected, with a deepening flush that broke slowly into streams of gold and fire. The climbing roses on their tall untidy arches were just touched to colour. Innocent, they looked, I thought, like children glad to know night safely behind them.

Near and far, the June landscape was now vocal with the exultant chorus of the birds, here in the terraced garden and away down into the low-misted Weald, where my old friend the milk-train was puffing away from Paddock Wood Station—no, it was much too soon for that, I remembered—it must be night's last goods-train which was going on its dilatory good-natured journey into the morning with that distant clink of buffers. Somehow the sound of it gave me a comfortable feeling of the world remaining pleasantly unchanged and peaceful. . . . The white pigeons too were already up and about, sitting idly on the gabled roof above their loft as though they didn't quite know what to do with themselves after getting up so early.

And now I was beholding the sun himself as his scarlet disc rose inch by inch above the auroral orchards and the level horizon far down the Weald. A very Kentish sun he looked, while I surmised, as had always been my habit, that he must be rising from somewhere just beyond Canterbury or the cliffs of Dover—rising out of the English Channel, in fact—this being as yet the boundary of my earthly adventures in that direction. There he was, anyhow, like some big farmer staring at his hay-fields and hop-gardens. And here was I, unconsciously lifting my arms to welcome the glittering shafts of sunrise that went wide-winged up through the innocent blueness above the east. But with the first rays slanting across the lawn everything somehow became ordinary again. On the tennis-court below, a busy little party of birds was after the worms. And I noticed that I'd forgotten to loosen the net when we'd finished yesterday evening's game. In the Arcadian cherry orchard across the road a bird-scaring boy had begun his shouting cries and clattering of pans. . . . I yawned; felt a bit lonely; and then went indoors to see if I could find myself something to eat.

## III

During these gentle revisitations of the days that are no more I sometimes enliven my imagination by resorting to an Ordnance Survey map of those parts of Kent and Sussex with which I am concerned. The Survey was made in 1866 and brought up to date and the map re-engraved in 1893; so it enables me to lose sight of the arterial road makings and other tyrannies of mechanized trafficry which have since altered the character of so much of the countryside. Far back in the '90's my mother had acquired it for finding her way to distant meets of the hounds; and in later years I myself never failed to unfold it after a day's hunting. It is therefore an old and valued friend, and no map could be more imbued with memorial associations and finger-marks.

My most recent porings over it have been for the purpose of measuring a few of the distances I drove with friends at whose houses I stayed for balls, in the days before motor-cars were much in use. For I was an enthusiastic dancer, though I can't claim ever to have been to more than about half-a-dozen important ones in a twelvemonth. An earnest rather than volatile performer with my patent-leather pumps, I never 'sat out' anything—not even 'The Lancers'—and I was hard at it until the band had played its final bar—unless some beckoning and unevadable chaperon decreed that her party must leave before the finish. 'Such a long way home for the horses' was the reason given for our reluctant departure—including the customary concession of 'Well, just *one* more, Marjorie, and that really must be the last'. And ten miles home on frosty roads frequently justified it.

'*Do you reverse?*' . . . How those words bring my silly self back to me, with my inability to make my white ties look as effortless as other young men's, and my white gloves which always would split in at least one place before the 'supper extras' emptied the floor for some really strenuous waltzing. I was particularly proud of my reversing, but I suspect that the young ladies found it a somewhat left-handed experience. One just went resolutely round the other way and made sketchy movements with the feet. 'The music seems to be playing specially for us, doesn't it?' murmured some light-footed partner, while we swayed to the soul-transporting strains of *Songe d'Automne*. And in my white simplicity I agreed with her, unaware that the remark was an artless variation of that traditional suggestion 'the world seems to have been made specially for us two! ' I remember one unromantic evening in a ballroom of Italianate design which contained a picture by Burne-Jones called ' The Hours '. The room was overcrowded, and while I bumped into people and apologized I was seldom unmindful of those languid and sedentary Praeraphaelite ladies who were presiding over our exertions—' wall-flowers ' they were, every one of them, like the shyly stoical girls whose programmes were so depressingly full of blanks.

' The Hours ' were six in number—just about the duration of the dance—and I have mentioned them because it now seems so peculiar that I should have been revolving beneath them for so many hours on end, and that I should now be putting their presence in my past on paper. One might be excused for moralizing about it. But the implications of the picture are obvious—many of the dancers and most—if not all—of the sedately watchful dowagers having since then asked for their carriages and departed for some destination beyond the reach of gilt-edged invitation cards. Would one willingly invite them back, to be as they then were in the world darkness of to-day? I cannot think so. And I remember—with a sigh—how more than once I have thought that it was well for my old friends that they went when they did.

Meanwhile I am still overhearing the muffled thrum and throb of music from ballrooms thirty years ago—overhearing, perhaps, that 'Blue Hungarian Band' which we all thought so wonderful. And I get a glimpse of myself, waiting impatiently for an overdue partner in some empty ante-room of mirrors that reflect my flushed and callow countenance. But the gaiety and the sentiment of what then was—do not these forbid me to make further game of old dancing days, reminding me, not of laborious toe-treading couples, but of those who took the floor triumphally and carried the music along with them in their controlled and graceful career—exemplifying, for older eyes that watched them, the momentary conquest of youth and the pathos of its unawareness?

Anyhow, here I am, with the dear old map yet again unfolded—quite in the mood to revisit one of those Queen Anne country houses where I awoke on the morning after a dance and drowsily observed the discreet man-servant putting a hot-water can into the hip-bath, wondering whether he was expecting me to give him half-a-sovereign or whether five bob would be decent, until he'd creaked away along the passage and I was up and looking out at frosted lawns and the sun just breaking through mist beyond the elm avenue. Revisiting some such house I should go there in summer—preferably on a dozy July morning. I should find myself in an upstairs room, leaning out of the tall sash-window from a sun-warmed window-seat. It is an unfrequented room, seeming to contain vibrations of vanished life. A summer room, too, where the cushions along the window-seat have had the colour faded out of them by many a morning such as this. Year after year the sunlight has come past half-drawn curtains to slant idly along the oak floor and up the panelled wall, at certain seasons creeping across the portrait above the fireplace—a girl in eighteenth-century dress with a little posy in her hands. ' The past is over and gone,' the sunlight seems to be saying, ' but the present is only that mottled butterfly fluttering dryly against the ceiling, and the old white pony pulling the mowing-machine to and fro on the lawn.' Down in the drawing-room the young lady of the house is practising Grieg's *Schmetterling* with rippling rapidity and a proper appreciation of its lyrical tenderness. And ' The past ought always to be like this ', I tell myself. ' Music with a heart-ache of happiness in it, overheard from the upstairs room of one's acquiescent mind, where the present is only waiting to become the past and be laid up in lavender for commemorative renewal.' But I must be getting back to realities again—or to such realities as I can muster-up from my obsolete Ordnance Map.

Meanwhile I will ask to be allowed to do it affectionately, taking my own time. Leaning on the sun-blistered white paint of the window-ledge, I must enjoy my final stare at the garden; listen to the stable clock striking twelve; hear the clink of a bucket as the stable-boy finishes washing the carriage-wheels, and then one of the horses neighing and snorting while the coachman goes to the corn bin with his sieve. From somewhere beyond a yew hedge comes a murmur of voices, talking contentedly as people do while sitting out of doors on a fine summer day—talking, I like to think, about the new standard roses which have done so well this year; with an afterword that perhaps it *would* be as well to have iced-coffee besides claret-cup for the small tennis party this afternoon. . . . And now I emerge from the upstairs room—a half-ghost, soundless from the shades of the future. Down the wide and slippery oak stairs I go, as I used to do when dressed and button-holed for a ball; and across the lofty panelled hall with its bland periwigged portraits and great open fireplace where huge smouldering logs sent out their pungent wood-smoke smell—that hall where I had danced Sir Roger de Coverley on stormy winter nights when I was only an awkward excited little boy. Then out by the big double doors, and away under the whispering trees, pausing near the homely farm buildings for a last look at the gracious red brick front of the house. Here it all is on my map; a name, and a few marks and dots; and just beyond the farm, the tiny river Bewlt joining the tiny river Teise.

For on the map they are both awarded the rank of River, though the youthful Bewlt in its five-mile wanderings had never been more than a brook; while the stripling Teise, which had yet another ten miles to travel before merging itself in the Medway at Yalding, was content to saunter past orchards, copses, pastures, and hop-gardens without achieving the dignity of working a water-mill or even earning a rent for its fishing-rights. I had never seen much of the Bewlt; but the windings of the Teise were well known to me, with the added interest that, for some seven miles before it met its tiny tributary, this pleasant alder-shaded stream formed the boundary between Kent and Sussex. The bit of it which I knew best was in Squire Morland's park at Lamberhurst, for it flowed past the fourth green of the nine-hole golf course, and many a time I had almost been into it with my second shot after topping my drive. And since the Teise was never more than a few miles from my home, I had always looked upon it as our local river, and as such had wished it well where it gurgled under little bridges.

Meanwhile I feel inclined to compare it—not only to this dallying digression—but also to the whole narrative thread of this discursive chapter. For I began my chapter with an unparticularized intention of amusing myself by memories of the adolescence of the auto-car; but I am already well away from the main roads, and glad of any excuse for continuing my journey by field paths and bridle tracks. 'For most, I know, thou lov'st retirèd ground' . . . I could quote several stanzas of *The Scholar Gipsy* in support of my propensity for meditative ramblings in the by-ways of my mind. I have never liked following the telegraph-poles on the straightest road to a populous destination. Give me the manor-farmstead that can only be reached after opening half-a-dozen gates, and the unassuming stream which never tells you what parish it intends to pass through next.

Squire Morland's park, which I mentioned not far back, provides yet another excuse for dawdling a bit longer in the vicinity of the river Teise. Some of my readers will recognize the scene, since I have described it—more briefly than it deserved—in an earlier volume of Memoirs. But that was fully a dozen years ago, so I may be forgiven this renewed retrospection of a place which I was fond of, and have always enjoyed thinking about. Let me add that although the course wasn't at all a good one I must have played many more rounds there than on any other. The worst thing about Lamberhurst golf was that it provided very poor practice for playing anywhere else. In fact one could almost say that it was 'a game of its own'. For one thing, you were perpetually hoicking the ball out of tussocky lies; and for another, the greens had justifiably been compared to the proverbial postage-stamp. If you pitched adroitly on to a green, it was more than likely that you wouldn't remain there. If, on the other hand, your ball fell short, you stopped where you were, which was in the rough grass. And the otherwise almost hazardless charm of our local links didn't always atone for these disadvantages, especially when one happened to be playing a medal-round at the Spring or Autumn Meeting. During the summer months the course got completely out of control and nobody bothered to play there except Squire Morland himself, and he had seldom done the nine holes in under fifty at the best of times. Go there on a fine April day, however, and there was nothing to complain of, provided that one gave the idyllic pastoral surroundings their due and didn't worry about the quality of the golf. I say ' pastoral ' because the place was much frequented by sheep, and I cannot visualize it without an accompaniment of bells and baa-ings.

Standing near the quiet-flowing tree-shaded river at the foot of the park, one watches a pottering little group of golfers moving deliberately down the south-westerly slope. It is one of those after-luncheon foursomes in which the Squire delighted; and there he is, playing an approach-shot to the third hole in that cautious, angular, and automatic style of his. The surly black retriever is at his heels, and his golf-bag has a prop to it, so as to save him stooping to pick it up, and also to keep his clubs dry. The clock on the village school strikes three, and one is aware of the odour of beer-making from the Brewery. The long hole to the farthest corner of the park is known as ' the Brewery Hole '. And now they are all on the green, and gallant old General Fitzhugh, who had conspicuously distinguished himself in the Afghanistan campaign some thirty years before, is taking tremendous pains over his put. The General has quite lately acquired one of those new Schenectady putters, mallet-shaped and made of aluminium, and popularized by Walter Travis, the first American who ever reached and won the Final of the Amateur Championship in England; and the non-success of his stroke is duly notified when he brandishes the weapon distractedly above his head. I now identify the stocky upright figure of my old friend Captain Ruxton, who evidently has ' that for it ', and sinks the ball with airy unconcern; whereupon the Squire, I can safely assume, ejaculates ' My word, that's a hot 'un, Farmer! ' in his customary clipped and idiomatic manner.

The fourth member of the party, I observe—unless one includes a diminutive boy from the village who staggers under the General's bristling armoury of clubs—is Mr. Watson, a tall, spectacled Scotsman, still in the prime of life, whose game is a good deal above Lamberhurst standards. Watson is a man well liked by everyone—without his ever saying much, possibly because he can't think of anything to say. My mother once remarked that when Mr. Watson ran out of small talk at a tea-party he told her that he always gave his hens salad-oil for the good of their health. But his favourite conversational opening was ' Have you been to Macrihanish? '—Macrihanish being an admirable but rather un-get-at-able golf course within easy reach of the Mull of Kintyre. A person of strict principles, he had never been heard to utter the mildest of expletives, even when he found one of his finest drives reposing in the footprint of a sheep. After making a bad shot he used to relieve his feelings, while marching briskly toward his ball, with a snatch of cheerful song. 'Trol-de-rol-de-rol' went Mr. Watson. But one had to have been to Macrihanish if one wanted to get much out of him in the way of conversation.

The friendly foursome is now well on toward the fourth green, where—in my mind's eye—I am standing by the tin flag, which requires repainting and has been there ever since the Club was founded. Following the flight of their tee-shots, I have remembered with amusement that Squire Morland occupies what might be called a duplicated position in the realms of print. His name appears, of course, in Burke's *Landed Gentry* and similar publications of lesser importance. But it also figures in *The Golfing Annual* as 'green-keeper to the Lamberhurst Golf Club'. (Nine holes. Subscription 21/- per annum.) The Squire's assumption of this sinecure appointment is due to the fact that by so doing he cannily obtains for himself and his cronies all the golf balls that he needs, at wholesale price. It is just conceivable that he does pull the light roller up and down about once a year; but I never heard of him doing so, though I myself had put in an hour's voluntary worm-cast sweeping now and again—the green-man being rather apt to neglect his duties.

In the meantime the foursome has another fourteen holes to play before it adjourns to the House for tea and a stroll in the garden to admire the daffodils. And while those kindly ghosts gather round me on the green I can do no more than wish that I could be greeting them there again, on some warm April afternoon, with the sheep munching unconcernedly and the course—as the Squire used to say—' in awful good condition '. But as the scene withdraws and grows dim I hear a blackbird warbling from the orchard on the other side of the river; and I know that his song on the springtime air is making even elderly country gentlemen say to themselves that one is only as old as one feels, especially when there is nothing forbidding about the foreground of the future—into which they are now, with leisurely solemnity, making ready to smite the ball.

## IV

I have already taken the liberty of remarking that Lamberhurst golf provided very poor practice for playing elsewhere. My 'elsewhere' in the fine April of 1910 was historic Westward Ho! There I played three full rounds daily during three consecutive weeks, Sundays excepted; and those fifty-four holes were an exacting journey, especially when one got into trouble among the clumps of head-high rushes in the middle of the round. 'How on earth did I do it?' I ask, seeing myself—after a hard single in the morning and a four-ball match on the top of a heavy lunch—chartering the assistant professional for yet another strenuous game, which would conclude when the sun had disappeared beyond Barnstaple Bay, and the actual position of the red flag on the eighteenth green was already becoming a matter for guess-work.

Glorious indeed, to be able to do that, and get up next morning fully resolved to do it again! But equally good, perhaps, to be able to put an equivalent amount of resolution into writing one's reminiscences, when one has ceased to have any golf handicap at all, and the courses one played on have been remodelled out of recognition, and the queer-shaped heads and hickory shafts of one's old set of clubs are as obsolete as the word 'foozle'. (I hope to be told that I am at fault in deploring the devaluation of 'foozle', for I have always liked it, in spite of its infelicitous associations.) It was, I think, the celebrated Andrew Kirkaldy who uttered that authoritative saying 'Gowf's a funny game!' So also is individual existence. And it is with the minutiae of mortality that I am mainly occupied in this half-humorous epitome of my career. What life means to the liver is much the same as what golf means to the golfer, who, like the rest of us, is decidedly dependent on the state of his health. And I take it—with a certain momentary sententiousness—to be highly significant of human affairs that a man like myself, who has done reasonably well in the arena of literature, should feel an almost equal regard for the sand-dunes among which he formerly straddled and swung and for those with whom he shared his enjoyment of the game. So to anyone who considers these golfing garrulities irrelevant to a literary autobiography I reply that they are included as evidence of my modest claim to be a transcriber of those oft-repeated words: *Homo sum; humani nil a me alienum puto.* To which I would add that when you get close up to life, little things are just as important as big ones.

I remember a huge sandy-haired Scotsman—wearing the somewhat tight and skimpy knickerbockers of the pre-plus-four period—who crouched over a two-foot put on the last green at Westward Ho! He had 'that to halve the match', and there was five bob on it. Happening to be his opponent, I watched him with hopeful anxiety, since his game was notorious for a combination of tremendous long hitting and pusillanimous putting. After an operose and portentous pause he somehow contrived to miss the hole. . . . Raising both freckled hands toward heaven, he exclaimed, with self-condoling emphasis, 'I did *not* deserve that!' In his opinion such treatment by fate was altogether unfair. 'But Maconachie,' I might well have remonstrated, 'you surely did deserve it, because you hit your ball wide of the hole.' Needless to say, I didn't; for I was about half his age. I merely pocketed two half-crowns and felt pleased. At the present moment, however, I see Maconachie as representative of the whole human race, accusing the unresponsive sky of having behaved unjustly when he has made a mistake for which he alone is responsible. And then walking resignedly toward the club-house to console himself with a long and oblivion-creating drink.

My friend Thompson, with whom I took my

golfing holidays when we were both in our early twenties, always remained philosophical when things went wrong with his game. Naturally, there were times when he became taciturn for a few holes; but he never went so far as refusing to answer a remark made with the object of easing the situation—which, I regret to say, I sometimes did.

When discussing old days, I have more than once reminded him of an incident—it was at Littlestone-on-Sea in the spring of 1908—when I discourteously declined to allow him a short but crucial put. Nonchalantly he knocked it in with one hand, and it leapt out of the tin, as such puts sometimes do. Unlike the aforementioned Maconachie he said nothing; but his demeanour demonstrated undisguised huffiness while we marched to the next tee, which was on the other side of a deep and wide dyke spanned by a single solid plank. Thompson's nailed shoes slithered on the rain-wet wood, and it was only after a series of acrobatic attitudes that he recovered his equilibrium. Years afterwards I asked him what the sequel would have been if he had fallen into those brown and brackish waters. 'I should certainly have returned to Cumberland by the next train', he replied, adding, 'With your usual tactlessness you'd have burst into a loud guffaw, and I was already simply paralytic with annoyance at missing the put—which you'd have given me if you'd possessed a spark of gentlemanly feeling! ' Whereupon I reminded him that the put was of paramount importance, for we were in the middle of the first round of our seventy-two-hole match on four consecutive courses. Littlestone, Rye, Sandwich, and Deal were the four, and the match was to decide, for the time being, which of us really was the sounder player. When crossing the dyke, Thompson was several holes up on me. But I am pleased to remember that I squared the match with a rather brilliant eighty-one at Rye. We left Sandwich still all square—Thompson's game having struck a bright patch after a couple of lessons from Tom Vardon, the professional there, who was a genially loquacious brother of the peerless Harry. At Deal, however, we found ourselves playing off the medal tees, and those long carries were too much for Thompson, who hadn't the physique for such heroic feats with a stiff breeze blowing. Also the new driver and brassy which he had hopefully acquired from Tom Vardon proved advantageous to me rather than to their owner; for some reason they caused him to produce low skimming shots—wind-cheaters, no doubt, but ineffective for outdistancing those Alp-like hazards into which he dourly descended to do battle with his heavy niblick. So I am obliged to record that our famous contest concluded disappointingly somewhere near the fourteenth green, where Thompson emerged from a deep bunker after a series of sandy explosions. And the only reason why the golden sovereign that he gave me isn't on my watch-chain is that I've never worn a watch-chain in my life. The coin would remind me—not only of our many happy days together—but also of the sterling metal of his character—a fact which nobody can be any the worse for hearing about, although its significance, like the result of our match, remains private and personal.

At Deal, by the way, we watched one of Harry Vardon's graceful victories, in a thirty-six-hole match against the burly Basque Frenchman Arnaud Massy, who, I think, tied with Vardon for the Open Championship in the following year and was defeated in the replay. Such a match would nowadays be followed by about ten thousand spectators; but on that pleasant breezy morning at Deal only a few hundred people were there, and the proceedings were in no danger of developing into a stampede. It was a decently-conducted game between two experts, and not an agglomeration of golf-ball advertisement and mass suggestion. But I must not give way to regretful thoughts on things as they were when famous golfers had yet to learn to play their strokes to the click of cameras. Rather must I rejoice that —until September, 1939—all forms of sport could attract a multiplicity of adherents, that the whole affair had become a sound commercial proposition for everyone concerned, and that the simplicity and vintage variety of games-playing had been superseded by a general uproar of unruminative technicality.

Nevertheless I retain a wistful regard for—among other matters—the county cricket I used to watch when I was young. The players all looked so unlike one another then; and there was an air of alfresco intimacy about their exploits which lent them a fuller flavour than seems perceptible now. For one thing, a fair number of obviously fat men were still taking plenty of wickets with slow medium-pace bowling. Quite comfortably corpulent some of them were, with impressive untrimmed moustaches which might sometimes be seen emerging from a tankard of beer in the pavilion. One of the stoutest bowlers I ever saw on the field was Baldwin of Hampshire. For some reason it gave me peculiar pleasure when I was told that in everyday life he was a wheelwright. It was nice to think of him making honest farm-waggons all the winter; and there was something about the way he hitched up his large loose trousers at the end of an over which made me see him standing outside an old workshop door daubed with the trial smearings of red, blue, and yellow paint that he'd used these many years on the wheels. But perhaps Baldwin wasn't a wheelwright after all, in which case I owe his rotund memory a respectful apology. Old Walter Humphreys, the Sussex lob-bowler, used to appear in a pale pink flannel shirt—made for him, I hope, by his wife—with an artfully flapping sleeve which deceived the batsman's anticipation of the break of the ball. It seemed more like home-made cricket in those days, and the people who played it really went home after the game, instead of—as one imagines now—being incorporated into the machinery of the popular Press. I have always maintained that the proper place for a first-class cricketer to achieve perpetuity is in *Wisden's Almanack*. Once there, he is academically preserved for future reference. If he chooses to be a wheelwright when away from the public eye it is nobody's business but his own, though the fact enriches his personality when divulged with decorum. And the stouter he is when nearing the age of retirement the better I like him. Even the slim, silk-shirted Ranjitsinhji had put on weight when he reappeared in his later years. The willowy magician had become an almost ponderous potentate.

As for W. G. Grace, the last time I beheld him he was trotting doggedly along behind a pack of foot-beagles; and while he pushed his way through a gap in a hedge I reverently computed that he must turn the scale at somewhere near fifteen stone.

* * *

Having got on to the pleasant subject of cricket, I may as well take the opportunity of saying a little more about my own doings in that serious pastime. By the season of 1910 I was playing regularly for the Blue Mantles Club, which had its headquarters on the county ground at Tunbridge Wells. There were—and still are, I believe—about thirty 'B-M. fixtures' in a season, and as about half of them were two-day matches I was able to get some good cricket. To be candid, the cricket was a good deal better than I was; but by being always available if someone 'chucked' I often obtained a place in the side at the eleventh hour. Certain of my fox-hunting friends, who were in the habit of following my performances in the club cricket reports of that long defunct daily *The Sportsman*, used to assert that my name always appeared as 'S. L. Sassoon did not bat'. That this was sometimes so I freely admit. But the Blue Mantles averages in my old scrap-book show that in the years 1910 and 1911 I had fifty-one innings, with ten not-outs, and an average of nineteen. This I consider quite a creditable record for a poet, and I don't mind saying that it gives me fully as much satisfaction as the royalty statements I have received from the publishers of my verse, some of which have been pecuniarily unimpressive. Anyhow, I am doing what I can to draw attention to my modicum of success at the wicket, there being no likelihood of anyone else doing it! I ought to add that the most eminent batsman who belonged to our club at that period was N. F. Druce, who had been top of the first-class averages as a young man, and had played five times for England versus Australia before his too early retirement from representative cricket. Referring to my scrap-book again, I find that in two seasons Druce scored nearly two thousand runs for us, with an average of eighty-six. To suggest, on statistics, that he was only about four times as good as I would be pretentious. The real difference between us was that while he, apparently, could make as many runs as he liked, I considered myself fortunate if I reached double figures. For his bat was like a barn-door, and the way he timed spin-bowling on a sticky wicket was a wonder to behold. To be appearing in the company of such a stylist was in itself something of an achievement, I used to think, when I was laboriously keeping my end up while he placed the ball where he pleased with juicy precision.

This brings me to a point where I feel that I must relate a little episode connected with motoring which I had in mind when—as I said some way back—I formed an unparticularized intention of making motor-cars the constructive theme of a chapter. Blue Mantle motorists were at that time still uncommon enough to be conspicuous. Druce owned a roomy car, and so did Osmund Scott, the famous golfer. 'Camel' Kelsey, who skippered the team, had also recently taken to this method of getting about, though he preferred old ways to new ones. Kelsey—a tremendous club cricketer—was tall and unhurrying, with a drawling, kindly voice. The voice was the man—uncensorious and totally likeable. I remember, by the way, that when I asked him how he enjoyed motoring he replied that the only thing against it was that it made his behind feel so tired; and I have since realized that there was a certain amount of truth in this observation. On the whole he liked walking better, and his long arms and sunbrowned face suggested that he would be no bad hand at scything a hayfield. There was something majestic about his deliberate movements, and he had made a century on almost every ground in Sussex. Other motorists there must have been, but the one who figures in the present anecdote was Captain Disney. Taller even than Kelsey, and resplendent in I Zingari colours, 'old Disney' as we called him—though he wasn't much over thirty at the time—was seldom absent from the team, in spite of twinges of rheumatism around the shoulders which caused him to talk gloomily about giving up the game. Disney was an essentially amiable character, but his demeanour gave one the impression that he found it difficult to take a rosy view of life as a whole. To watch him when he went on to bowl was a recurrent comedy, especially in dull and chilly weather. With an air of Hamlet-like infestivity he would skin-off his two sweaters, spin his arm stiffly a few times, indicate sadly to some of the fielders that they might as well get a bit deeper and prepare for the worst, and finally deliver the widest of wides. I must however do Disney justice by adding that he was a tolerably effective trundler when he had got warmed up to it; and his batsmanship was done in the grand style—left leg and shoulder well forward and a fine follow-through.

He had impressed me as having a touch of the artistic temperament about him—in fact it had come to my knowledge that he was something of an amateur musician—so it was quite a surprise when he broke new ground by appearing as the earnest advocate of an invention which, according to him, was going to revolutionize tyre-trouble. He told everyone about it, non-motorists such as myself included. Its name, if I remember rightly, was 'Proofax'. And if it wasn't, I can only say that it ought to have been, because it had yet to prove its efficaciousness. Like all great inventions it was perfectly simple. You merely pumped it into people's tyres, and—to paraphrase a line of Praeraphaelite poetry—they drew it in as simply as their breath. What they drew in, through Disney's zealous agency, was a forbidding-looking fluid which resembled liquid tar, or better still, black molasses—molasses being a word which suggests consistent stickiness. Meanwhile old Disney, with the full force of his sincerity, proceeded to urge the adoption of his puncture panacea upon all who arrived at Blue Mantle matches in motor-cars. The main merit claimed for 'Proofax' was that, once safely inside the inner-tube, it neither liquefied nor solidified, as some substances might have done, but retained its puncture-proofing properties in all their original non-corrosive consistency for an indefinite period. When pressed to reveal exactly how long it *would* last, Disney replied, with a certain evasiveness, that it would last as long as the inner-tube did. It was, in fact, practically guaranteed to prolong rather than lessen the life of inner-tubes, thus combining comfort with economy. My old friend Fred Buzzaway (number ten or eleven on the Blue Mantle batting order and a rather bow-legged runner after the ball) was heard to remark, in his usual knowing way, that Master Disney's sticky stuff might be a workable proposition now, but how would it be shaping by the end of next hunting season? He added that in his humble opinion it would soon be carrying a breast-high scent. But Fred was inclined to be sceptical about most things, barring his own ability to see the end of a good hunt, whether he was grinning along after the Burstow Hounds on his old horse or acting as an honorary whipper-in to the Hadlow foot-harriers.

Anyhow, in the first flush of his persuasiveness Disney induced some of our team to submit their wheels to his experiment. Druce, with his customary good-nature, was one of them. Conan Doyle—who still turned out occasionally, though his batting was rather on its last legs and his artful slows had lost their former effectiveness—gave 'Proofax' his august consideration but decided against it, no chemical analysis being forthcoming; while Kelsey announced that he preferred fresh air to treacle in his tyres. Disney then applied himself to visiting teams. I used to observe him in serious confabulation with someone during the luncheon-interval; and soon, if the notion had been favourably received, he would produce the apparatus from his own car at the back of the pavilion and become busy with what must have been some sort of re-adapted foot-pump. He was a bit aloof toward anyone who went to watch, but there was usually an interested little knot of onlookers around him, offering advice and encouragement while he pumped away for all he was worth, straightening himself up now and again to reassure the optimistic owner of the tyres that 'Proofax' was the brightest idea of the century. And when the job was completed and the match at an end he probably told the departing driver that if he returned next season he wouldn't have had any cause to complain about punctures. By the next cricketing season, however, Disney had discarded his patent pump and no longer carried cylinders of 'Proofax' about in the back of his car. If anyone mentioned the matter—and Fred Buzzaway did so more than once—he affected a melancholy unconcern. The truth was that something in the nature of spontaneous combustion had supervened. What else could one call it, when Norman Druce had found himself spinning along a lonely road with both back tyres spouting a lava-like substance, reported, perhaps inaccurately, to have been actually luminous? And one of someone else's front tyres had unluckily exploded just as his wife's mother was stepping in to go to some swell garden-party.

## V

In this ' real autobiography ' of mine I have hitherto done what I could to avoid the subject of fox-hunting, for the excellent reason that it has already been monopolized by a young man named George Sherston. To tell the truth, I am a little shy of trespassing on Sherston's territory. I should not like to feel that I had in any way impaired his reality in the minds of his appreciative friends, for many of whom he is, perhaps, more alive than the present writer. And to assert that he was ' only me with a lot left out ' sounds off-hand and uncivil. There is also the problem of his Aunt Evelyn, a lady whom I couldn't possibly run the risk of offending, although she was never one to complain about being asked to take a back seat.

But here we are, all the same, back in the spring of 1911. And there is young George, lugging the garden roller to and fro on the tennis lawn after tea, while the birds warble and scold among the laurels and arbutuses in the lengthening March twilight. There he is, intensively pondering on his chances of winning the Heavy Weight Race down in Sussex a few weeks hence. And there is Aunt Evelyn, tinkling ' The Harmonious Blacksmith ' on the drawing-room piano and wishing, in her heart of hearts, that point-to-point races had never been invented. There, likewise, is the Weald of his youth, its heart-holding distances finding gradual forgetfulness in twilight, while those hill-top trees over at Gedges Farm stand dark and distinct against the embers of a serenely clouded sunset. Such being so—and the pleasure of renewing acquaintance with old friends not a thing to be undervalued—let me suppose that Miss Sherston has been asked to stay with us for as long as she chooses, and that George has been somehow mysteriously embodied in his author. For I must say I like to think of grey-haired Aunt Evelyn coming out into the garden with my mother to remind me that it is almost time to dress for dinner; and after all she is just the sort of lady who might quite well be staying with my mother —in fact I could swear that I've seen them sitting with their sunshades up while I was batting in one of our village matches, talking about politics and gardening until their straying attention is recalled to the game by the termination of my innings. 'O dear, he's got out! How tiresome!' exclaims my mother in the middle of an incisive denouncement of the maddening behaviour of the Liberal Party or the 'Little Englanders', or an anxious inquiry as to how much Aunt Evelyn's fruit blossom suffered from those late spring frosts. But I must return to my roller, which has been revolving, as usual, with a subdued screeching and an occasional groan, suggesting the need of oil in its well-weathered anatomy. And while I go up and down the lawn for what really must be the last time unless I am to be late for dinner, let none of us doubt that dear Aunt Evelyn is getting herself ready in the best bed-room and wondering why fine mild evenings at the end of March always take one back to the days when one was a girl. It must be because of the window being wide open, and the thrushes singing so beautifully loud and clear in the twilight. Or perhaps it's the thought of everything being out again soon and spring just as wonderful as ever. How quickly the years do slip away as one gets older, she muses, remembering how little George came running out into the garden to tell her so excitedly that the Prince of Wales had won the Derby, while she was cutting some white lilac down by the bee-hives. ' That was before I moved the hives to the apple-orchard ', she reminds herself. ' Nearly fifteen years ago now; and George was just growing out of his first riding-suit. ' . . . With a gentle sigh she picks up a tortoise-shell-backed hair-brush, rebuking herself for being so dilatory as she hears the gong going for dinner.

Having thus ushered out my dilemma (which was a collision between fictionized reality and essayized autobiography) I can now proceed with equanimity to an account of my first two appearances as a race rider.

In the previous December I had bought my eight-year-old horse Cockbird from a hard-riding youth whose father had been a hunting-field crony of my mother's. For the time being all other interests were out-weighed by my anxious ambition to win a point-to-point. Our groom Richardson had complete confidence in him. The only uncertainty in his mind—and my own—was whether I was a strong enough rider to hold him together and keep him up to his fences. It is also conceivable that we shared a horrid doubt whether I should be in the saddle at all by the end of a race. Cockbird, by the way, had only one imperfection, though I wasn't aware of it until I had ridden him in several races. But I must begin by enumerating his merits. He was extremely good-looking, and possessed all the points which go to make a first-rate hunter. His beautiful sloping shoulders were in themselves a guarantee that he would give one a comfortable ride, and his action was so smooth that one scarcely felt him moving while he galloped. When he came to a fence he shortened his stride and slipped over it, always jumping very big and getting away with unfaltering fluency after he landed. Besides being a natural jumper he had a perfect mouth, going well into his bridle without ever seeming to catch hold. He was, in fact, a 'patent safety', and had a fine constitution which enabled him to do a long day's hunting without ever seeming tired or being any the worse for it afterwards. His one weak point was that he didn't finish well in a race. He had apparently come to the conclusion that when he had jumped the last fence there was no further need to hurry. What did it matter, thought Cockbird—who gave one an impression of being a somewhat museful character—whether someone else passed the winning-post in front of him? He had completed the course in his usual artistic style, so why need he take it out of himself any more? In other words he lacked the competitive spirit, and preferred cantering in with dignity to hurrooshing home in a mad rush for victory. I must add that toward the end of his point-to-point racing career he took to trying to run out left-handed into the crowd after sailing over the last obstacle, and more than once I came up the straight with all my weight on the right rein! Had he been a really high-couraged horse we should have won more races than we did. But as things were he was what I needed—a thoroughly easy animal to ride—and I can never be too grateful for the vicarious credit which he earned me. Altogether I rode him in eleven races, of which he won four, was once second, and three times third. And in four hunting seasons he only gave me two falls, one at a big fence where he had a glare of evening sun in his eyes, and the other when he landed over a hairy hedge on to the stump of a willow. All of which proves conclusively that it was a lucky day for me when I got him for fifty pounds owing to a vet having asserted that he was a slight whistler —an accusation which turned out to be unfounded. And now, having given my old quad a good 'write up', I must ask the reader to accompany me to the saddling-enclosure where Richardson is strenuously tightening the girths, while I do my utmost to look pleased at being about to make my débût, in the Open Race at the Ashford Valley Harriers Meeting.

The feel of it all comes back to me as though it had happened only yesterday. . . . The mild grey afternoon with its low sagging clouds; the smell of trampled grass, and the clamour of bookies bawling the odds; the yawning intestinal trepidation; and the ebbing aplomb with which I entered the weighing-tent to be jostled by the good humoured robustness of more experienced riders.

And the background of being among a crowd of people none of whom took more than a casual interest in me as they consulted their race-cards and passed on to have a look at the favourite. An epitome of a young man's existence, one might moralize. Remembering it, I wish that it might happen all over again, just for a glimpse of the suppressed anxiety and restrained satisfaction on Richardson's keen-featured countenance, just for a taste of the excitement and uncertainty which can never be the same after one has ridden away from one's youth. Of the actual race not much need be written. There were eight runners, four of whom were previous winners, so I was in quite good company. As detailed in my hunting diary the course was a fairly easy one, though the going was heavy after much recent rain. 'Was well with them until half way round and then eased him a bit; got fifty yards behind the first three and couldn't catch them up again. Finished fourth.' Such was my way of describing the event; but it would have been more accurate to say that by half way round I was out of breath and very numb in the arms, and thereafter allowed Cockbird to canter along at his ease—my main object being to complete the course without mishap. Richardson, however, appeared to be quite satisfied with the result, and remarked that the old chap would be a stone better for the gallop. And my own sensations might be summarized as a state of enraptured relief at having got round without actually making a fool of myself. By an unavoidable coincidence it happened to be my mother's birthday—unavoidable being the right word, because she would obviously have preferred not to be spending the afternoon on tenterhooks of anxiety. Anyhow I returned to Ashford—the only poet in a bus-load of bookmakers—and the train took me home feeling that I might have done very much worse. My mother was delighted to hear that I'd 'come in fourth'—and even more delighted, I suspect, that I'd come back without any broken bones.

* * *

Meanwhile I must explain that the race which, like Sherston, I was hoping to win was the Southdown Members Heavy Weights. This should have been run about ten days after the Ashford Valley, but the clerk of the weather intervened with a series of snow-storms, and the country became so waterlogged that the meeting was postponed for a fortnight. I had, however, also entered for the West Kent Open Race on April 19th, and Richardson now regarded this as an appropriate winding-up to Cockbird's preparation for 'the Cup' which I was prayerfully proposing to carry home from Sussex. I myself was in strict training, and hadn't smoked my pipe for a month.

That year the West Kent Races were at Ide Hill, which was about fifteen miles from us, at the far end of the Weald, toward London. Two days before the event I bicycled over for a cogitative walk round the course. It was a cloudless afternoon; the bluebells were out in the oak-woods and every bank was alight with primrose bunches. But what cared I for wild flowers? The fact that the ground was at last drying up nicely was all that mattered to me, since this, I knew, would suit Cockbird better than deep going. 'What shall I be feeling like this time on Wednesday?' was the refrain of my thoughts as I free-wheeled down the steep hill to Scallop's Farm and caught sight of the large tent for the Farmers' Lunch and the red and white flags in the fields and hedges below.

Walking round the course took less time than I'd expected. The fences weren't at all alarming; and there were, if I remember rightly, only fourteen of them, all artificially constructed for the occasion. We had to go round twice, which I calculated to make not more than three miles, if as much. The Southdown course, which I had more or less committed to memory earlier in the month, was almost a mile longer, and over what was practically a natural hunting country. This one struck me as being not much more than a gallop round. Cockbird would make light of it. A few stiff stake-and-binders would have been to his advantage, I thought, eyeing the neat little brush fences with condescension. There was only one place which caused me to stop and ponder its possibilities. Coming at the tenth fence one had to make a sharp turn round a flag. The fence itself was nothing to worry about, but it was just the sort of awkward bend where a horse might run out. 'Now this is where you've got to go steady and make no mistake about it,' I warned myself, regarding the flag-pole inimically. I then sauntered down the hill to have another look at the water-jump, a mere show-ring affair which Cockbird would fly with yards to spare. And most of the way home, on the almost empty roads of thirty years ago, I was wondering what it would really feel like to ride a winner. All that evening, too, I was mentally steering my mount round the course, every detail of which was clearly impressed on my enthusiastic brain.

Driving over to Ide Hill thirty-six hours later, with the stable-boy sitting awe-struck on the back-seat of the dog-cart, my sensations of anxiety prevented any kind of coherent thought. In the fine April weather I was journeying toward my fate along a dusty road. Birds were singing, and 'all nature seemed smiling and gay'; but the only thing my mind could be positive about was that it wouldn't even be safe for me to consume my ham-and-tongue sandwiches, since my race wasn't till 2.45, and it would never do to risk eating anything before then. The first race was at 1.15. After that there was a long luncheon-interval, during which I should be obliged to wander emptily about while everyone else munched sociably in the golden sunshine. At the end of my two-hour drive there was at any rate the portentous interest of buying a card and perusing the entries. This, however, took only a few seconds to do, though it provided food for thought. There were but four competitors in the Open Race. *Mr. C. Leveson-Gower's Peacock* turned up afterwards as a post-entry, which didn't increase my chances of winning—he being a very well-known rider. In the meantime *Mr. H. Buckland's Cocky* would be more than enough to go on with! I had watched Cocky win easily at the Ashford Valley Races; and Harry Buckland himself was a more than local horseman; in fact he held the world record for high jumping, a feat which he had performed at Olympia on a horse which he had trained for Walter Winans, a renowned American millionaire who drove fast-trotting horses in spider buggies, had a grey goatee beard, and was reputed to be one of the finest revolver shots in the universe. I had seen him at a sumptuous hunt-breakfast which he had given for the Stag Hounds at his house near Ashford. Of *Mr. T. Kirby Stapley's Ladybird* I knew nothing beyond the fact that Mr. Stapley was the popular Master of the East-bourne Foxhounds, to which he acted as amateur huntsman. Less formidable than Buckland, he was known as a difficult man to beat, as I discovered twelve months later when he defeated my old horse Rubicon by a length at the East Sussex point-to-point, sitting like a sack of coals, but riding Ladybird a real whirlwind finish. My third opponent on the card was a cavalry captain whose horsemanship I had good reason to respect, since I had recently seen him ride a winner at a military meeting in East Kent. To-day he had entered a horse of his own called *Starlight*.

'Poof!' I thought—if 'Poof' can claim to be included in the category of thinking—'It really does seem extraordinary—me competing against all these terrific nuts!' But when I sought Richardson's opinion of our chances of beating Buckland he merely replied that Cocky would be carrying a fourteen-pound penalty and our horse would make him gallop whatever happened. Richardson was enjoying every minute of it and feeling much more important than I was. He had ridden Cockbird over the day before and they had spent the night at Scallop's Farm. 'He knows what's on all right!' he now remarked, with grim gleefulness, as he rubbed away at Cockbird's quarters where he had broken out in a sweat of excitement. Richardson didn't even bother to ask what I'd done with the dog-cart and the stable-boy, whom I'd left to find what accommodation he could when I lugged my kit-bag to the dressing-tent, wondering the while whether anyone was mistaking me for a hard-boiled gentleman rider. (I had bought the kit-bag second-hand, so it looked quite respectably old.)

It was not yet one o'clock; but Richardson wasn't in a mood to waste words, so I decided that I might as well go and change into my boots and breeches. I had no intention of concealing from the public the fact that I was 'having a bump round'; and while walking about in a state of acute suspense it would afford me a modicum of self-satisfaction to be recognized as a rider, though very few people would know or care who I was. When the first race was over I wandered aimlessly among the crowd, a fair proportion of whom had disappeared into the Farmers' Lunch tent, from which they would convivially emerge to back old Cocky down to an odds-on favourite. During my uneasy perambulations I wished that I knew some of the West Kent people personally. I had only hunted with them a few times and had usually been too shy to speak unless spoken to, which had mainly consisted in being 'capped a quid' by the hunt secretary as a non-subscriber. So it took me quite by surprise when a genial red-faced man in a grey bowler, apparently knowing me better than I knew him, hailed me from one of the farm waggons drawn up alongside the straight finish of the course, and invited me to hop up and have a bite of lunch. The party of people on the waggon were all as jolly as could be, and before I knew where I was I had put myself outside some appetizing sandwiches and had been provided with a glass of champagne. I couldn't help wondering whether this mightn't be bad for my wind; but it would have been ungracious to refuse, and breakfast now seemed a long time ago. Also it was a relief not to be parading up and down like a spirit on the shores of the Styx, with one of my boots beginning to give me a blistered heel into the bargain. Sipping my champagne, which was in rather a big glass, I chatted with confiding candour to an amiable lady who showed much interest in Cockbird and his prospects of doing well in the Open Race. And by the time I looked at my watch and found that I ought to go and get ready, point-to-point racing had become a free-and-easy and almost festive occupation. Good wishes accompanied my departure, and altogether I was quite a different person when I rejoined Richardson and the race-horse.

No longer feeling the least bit nervous, I passed through my preliminaries with positive jauntiness—even going so far as to bid a facetious farewell to the clerk of the scales, to the effect that I was hoping to see him again later on if I hadn't broken my neck in the meantime. Finally, in the full flush of steeplechasing publicity, I was given a leg-up into the saddle by the stable-boy. Cockbird, too, was very much on his toes, and had never looked more muscular in his life. 'They won't catch me getting left behind this time!' I thought, as I cantered down the straight with a bumping heart, in what I believed to be workmanlike style, eyeing the great Harry Buckland on his iron-mouthed old black horse, who wasn't much to look at but could do a hard season with the Stag Hounds and the Harriers and come out in April to win two or three races. A minute later we were lined up, and the starter on his strawberry roan cob gave us the word 'Go!' And go

I did, with airy impetuosity; for, as will already have been surmised, that beaker of ' bubbly ' had effectively dissolved my diffidence. Cockbird, steered rather than controlled by his volatile rider, showed quite a turn of speed, flicking the fences behind him in his usual ground-gaining way. I was, in fact, making the pace for the others; and so hot did I make it that we were two fields ahead of them at the ninth fence. Buckland, no doubt, was watching my spurt with sagacious amusement and waiting for it to die away. But Cockbird was a stayer, and I still think that my lead might have been a winning one if I'd kept steadily on. I am, indeed, human enough to feel persuaded that, could I but transfer my mellowed and experienced self from this chair to that saddle, the result of the race would have been different. All, however, after that ninth fence, was exactly what it ought not to have been! My mental stereoscope reveals me going harum-scarum across a large flat field, rapidly approaching the flag-pole at which I had so seriously warned myself to exercise discretion. It was then that I should have taken a resolute pull at my horse and concentrated my whole mind on collecting him for the leap, after passing as near the flag-pole as possible. But I wasn't concentrating on anything. I was merely glorying uncollectedly in the fact that the others were such a long way behind—so far behind that, after I'd gone irreparably wide of the flag and been conveyed clean out of the course, Cockbird, who could be extremely nappy when annoyed, had time to refuse the fence two or three times before the others came along to give him a lead. That he finished the course in faultless style was no consolation. Behind them I went in forlorn and desperate pursuit for the remainder of the race. Buckland beat Stapley by half a length, and I passed the champagne waggon fifth of the five. Richardson met me with a philosophic smile. When I had explained how it had happened, omitting the champagne, he told me not to be downhearted about it. 'Just wait till Saturday and see if we don't have a bit of luck,' he remarked.

He was right. We did have a bit of luck, and I came home with my first point-to-point cup. . . . But all that has already been told in detail by my prototype George Sherston. He, however, when describing his victory on Cockbird in the Sussex Weald, said nothing at all about his unlucky day in the west of the Weald of Kent.

## VI

Although I had always regarded the writing of poetry as a thing which needed to be kept to oneself, I now began to feel that it would be to my advantage if I were a little less remote from the literary world. I often wished that I could make friends with some other poets, but I never seemed to get any nearer to knowing any of them.

A few weeks after the sporting events described in my preceding chapter something happened which appeared likely to produce hopeful results. My mother and I were invited to an afternoon party at the Edmund Gosses'. There, at any rate, I should get a look at Mr. Gosse himself.

I have already made mention of his cordial letter in response to my *Orpheus in Diloeryum*. Toward the end of 1909 I had followed this up by sending him my *Sonnets*, drastically revised and rather sumptuously reprinted from the destroyed edition, and had received a long reply in his graceful and delicate handwriting. The Librarian of the House of Lords, though—as he expressed it—' in the depths of public business ' when my thin quarto reached him, had spared himself no effort in offering advice and encouragement. He had even ' found four lines in these few poems which are absolutely impossible to scan without an offence against language '. One of the lines was ' No infinite chasms of space beyond your mastery '. I myself had thought this interpolated alexandrine impressive; but I decided that it didn't lose much when I cut out ' infinite ', though I suspected that ' chasms ' ought not to be a two-syllable word. It seemed that I must be less slap-dash in future, for Mr. Gosse had concluded by hoping that in these days of outrage I should defend the purity of the English language—a responsibility for which I was as yet altogether unprepared.

Meanwhile there was the prospect of the afternoon party, which was to be given—as Mrs. Gosse explained in her letter to my mother—' for our old friend Maarten Maartens '. Of this eminent author I knew no more than that he was a Dutchman who wrote in English. My mother had read *God's Fool*, one of his best-known novels, and described it as powerful but rather unpleasant. But I was mainly interested in the possibility of meeting one or two famous poets. My mother, though she always enjoyed what she called ' seeing the dressy London ladies ', would probably have been quite glad to exchange the party for one of Mrs. Gosse's too infrequent visits to Weirleigh.

She had come to us for a few days in the previous summer, and the aristocratic white-painted seat which she had sent us afterwards had found its proper place in the garden, with a yew hedge behind it and that north-west outlook across the Weald which could be so deeply and memorably blue. But it was high time the dear thing came and sat on her seat, remarked my mother, adding that the blackbirds and thrushes seemed to have decided that it had been put there specially for them to call on, since they were always leaving yewberry cards on it.

Mrs. Gosse, when she came to stay with us, brought very little of the literary world with her. In fact one could almost say that the only professional writer about whom she 'spoke on purpose' was Mr. Gosse. The others—Henry James and Thomas Hardy for instance—she merely mentioned by accident (and at that time I hadn't read a word by either of them). What I had so far gleaned about 'Edmund' was a fragmentary impression of someone reading aloud to her in resonant tones, which she imitated appreciatively while telling us how, when struck by a fine passage in some old author, he liked to roll it forth to her from the table at which he worked. I also inferred that he could be delightfully gay and diverting, and more than once she gave a glimpse of him being rather comically fidgety and impatient. ' What a *caution* he is! ' she exclaimed, with the tolerant affection of one who had for thirty-five years been the background of his active and zestful existence. She herself was one of the least fussy people I had ever known. Her voice was richly subdued and reassuring, and there was a sense of security in all that she did. Like all the best women, she had an element of masculinity in her. The bigness of her nature was visible in the cast of her features, which were noble without being perfect in their proportions.

When Mrs. Gosse came to the country she made us feel homelier than ever, for she asked nothing better than to have a good comfortable gossip with ' Trees ', as she called my mother. Their voices murmured endlessly on while they cruised about the garden or sat in the alcove by the vinery. My mother did most of the talking. It was such a relief to be with a real fellow creature, she said. Mrs. Gosse fanned herself and listened and looked at the view. She was always a great one for fanning herself, even when the temperature wasn't noticeably warm! She would watch a long afternoon of lawn tennis with an air of lulled contentment, forgetting the crowd of famous conversationalists and the ceaseless industry of Mr. Gosse's career and the round of domestic duties which she had left behind her in London. I remember how interested she became when I told her that I was going to the Canterbury Cricket Week Ball. It was almost as if she wished she were going there too. I don't suppose that there had been many dancing men or lawn tennis players among the poets and painters with whom she had mingled since her art-student days in the early '70's, when my mother used to skate with her on the Serpentine and take her to the Paddington Baths. 'Trees was such a splendid swimmer,' she remarked, 'but I never could learn to dive though she often tried to teach me.' It was difficult to imagine Mrs. Gosse plunging into a swimming bath; but she seemed to me exactly right as she was—kind and humorous and undeviatingly reliable.

* * *

During my dreamy boyhood I had thought of Edmund Gosse as a being who—as he might himself have put it—'existed solely in an enraptured atmosphere of Heliconian enchantments'. In other words I imagined him only in ideal association with poets and poetry. My earliest perusals of *Gossip in a Library* and *Critical Kit-Kats* had made me vaguely responsive to the vintage flavour of his style and the gusto of appreciation which he communicated so gracefully. For the great thing about him was that he really made one want to read the authors about whom he wrote. I cannot claim that he actually induced me to study any of the books he discussed, but he made me think how pleasant it would be to do so, which was—at fourteen years old—quite good enough for a start. My liking for bygone books undoubtedly began when I read about Gerard's *Herbal* and Camden's *Britannia* in *Gossip in a Library*. I sniffed the aroma of old leather bindings, and foresaw myself as the owner of a noble array of dim-gilt folios. I knew of him as a distinguished critic of contemporary writing, but I preferred to forget that it was sometimes his duty to be displeased. The Gosse of my unimpeded reveries concerned himself with nothing less delectable than a peach picked from a sun-warmed wall. He lived in a long summer afternoon where authors, like bees, were busy among the flowers of speech. And this charmed conception of him I still more or less retained even in my twenty-fifth year. The poems of his intimate friend Austin Dobson, with their old-world quality and delicate feeling, had contributed to this impression. I may have dimly realized that for many years the two of them had been colleagues at the Board of Trade, but if I did so I was able to put the matter out of my mind. His own collection of accomplished and melodious verse, *On Viol and Flute*, did nothing to diminish my idea of him as what I can only call 'a fragrant personality'. The very buckram in which his books were bound—it was a brownish-red which had mellowed pleasantly in fading—was connected in my mind with a portly jar of pot-pourri that stood near the set of book-shelves in our drawing-room—shelves which contained my mother's flower books, the Waverley Novels, Miss Austen, *Barchester Towers*, and other special favourites of hers. Among them was a small volume of minor verse called *Dreams to Sell*. Since my childhood this name had evoked an indefinite chord from the small Aeolian harp of my sensibility, though I had never bothered to look at any of the poems. It was only when I came to read Mr. Gosse's essay on Beddoes that the origin of the title became known to me.

> *If there were dreams to sell*
> *What would you buy?*
> *Some cost a passing bell,*
> *Some a light sigh*
> *That shakes from Life's fresh crown*
> *Only a rose-leaf down.*

There, perhaps, in the rose-leaf of that lyric, I now discover the clue to my conjunction of the buckram binding with my mother's pot-pourri. And I think that Mr. Gosse himself would have thought none the worse of me had he known that I was in the habit of associating him and his works with embalmed rose-petals and lavender. His gratified amusement might, however, have led to his reminding me that other persons existed for whom his name signified gall, wormwood and vinegar! But in 1911 I was still unaware of his rather easily provoked literary animosities and temporary vendettas. Nor had I read his prose masterpiece *Father and Son*, though it had been published several years before. There I should have seen him at his best.

The fact that he had been my Uncle Hamo's best friend was too much of a family affair to be amalgamated with my luminous day-dreams. But while rummaging in one of the studio ottomans I had lately discovered a photograph of Uncle Hamo's wedding group, and Mr. Gosse was in it as 'best man', though I didn't identify him for certain until I had consulted my mother. He looked earnest and not very remarkable, with a low turn-down collar and a funny little bow-tie. But that was in 1883. He had looked more mellow and distinguished when I saw him at the dance in Hampstead Town Hall twenty years later—an episode which I have described in a previous chapter. On the whole, therefore, it was a somewhat idealized Edmund Gosse whom I now looked forward to meeting at the afternoon party in Hanover Terrace.

★ ★ ★

It might have been expected that we should arrive at the Gosse 'At Home' punctually—or even too early. But for some reason we didn't. It may have been that we spent the first part of the afternoon at the Royal Academy Exhibition, which my mother always 'went round' with time-forgetting energy and intentness. At any rate the party was in full swing when we made our inconspicuous entry. My appearance, I felt, was creditable enough, for I was wearing my buff linen waistcoat, with spats to match, and there was nothing countrified about my irreproachable dark summer suit. Thus attired, I ought to have had a self-possessed and reticently distinguished personality; but even my best clothes could not prevent me from being excessively shy and self-conscious.

From time to time my friend Tessa Gosse did what she could by presenting me to a series of apparently non-literary ladies whose names I didn't quite catch; but none of them succeeded in putting me at my ease, and it seemed that I had come to the party mainly to utter flat remarks about the Coronation, which was to be about a month later. 'Will you be in London for the Coronation?' I laboriously inquired, readily agreeing when they responded by saying that on the whole it would be just as well not to be. (It was obviously no use telling them that I was booked to play for the Blue Mantles against Upper Tooting on Coronation Day, though I can now record that there was no cricket after lunch owing to heavy rain.)

I should have liked to ask them not only who they were but who everybody else was; but one couldn't do that with people to whom one had only just been introduced. That bearded man with the large jovial laugh who was hob-nobbing with my mother on a sofa—could he be Alma-Tadema? I wondered. And if so, was she talking to him about his picture of Moses among the Bulrushes —a work from which he had for once omitted his usual flight of marble steps? Other men standing about conversing with easy unconcern might possibly be publishers, or even editors, but none of them looked like poets. There was one little incident which made me feel more my natural self; this was when Mrs. Gosse, who was moving about in her unruffled way, paused beside me and drew my attention to a voluminous middle-aged lady in a huge feathery hat. 'That is "Answer me with those azure eyes",' she murmured, with subdued playfulness in her look, recalling to my mind the American poetess of whom she had spoken last summer, whose exuberant admiration for Mr. Gosse had caused her to address him thus in a sonnet.

So far my own eyes had caught but an occasional glimpse of Mr. Gosse, who was very evidently in the throes of acting the host as he darted about in ardent redistribution of his guests. Me, alas, he had not redistributed—or even greeted. But while I was conducting one of my transitory feminine acquaintances toward the tinkle of teaspoons down in the dining-room I encountered him, much engrossed in guiding a pink and glossy gentleman up the stairs. A few moments later I was able to observe that he stopped outside the drawing-room door to point out and explain a picture (which I now know to have been the original of Pellegrini's famous Vanity Fair cartoon of Swinburne as a young man). I had not noticed the picture, but it was impossible not to overhear Mr. Gosse repeatedly and effusively addressing his guest as 'Your Excellency'. So that was something to take home with me, I thought. I had heard Mr. Gosse doing the polite to an Ambassador—probably the Dutch one, since the party was given in honour of a Dutch author. Nevertheless it wasn't what I'd been expecting of him, and I felt dimly disappointed.

It was with some such feeling that, when the crowd in the drawing-room had begun to dissolve, I slipped out on to the balcony. Leaning on the balustrade I stared across the greenery of Regent's Park, which looked gaily Arcadian in the brilliant May sunshine. The polite hubbub of the party having abated, I could hear what I took to be the roaring of the lions at the Zoo, which was only about half-a-mile away. Probably it was feeding-time, I thought. Meanwhile there was plenty of time yet before we needed to go and catch our train, and it was a relief to be alone with my confused awareness that so far it had all been unlike what I had hoped for. I had imagined that I should meet—or at least overhear—one or two celebrated literary personages, but there had been nothing noteworthy except Mr. Gosse and ' Your Excellency ', plus the languishing American poetess, who was evidently not to be taken seriously.

My brief meditation was pleasantly interrupted by the arrival of Mrs. Gosse with her quiet-voiced ' Ah, there you are, dear! Come in and be introduced to Dr. van der Poorten-Schwarz and his daughter Ada '. This was the first I'd heard of the real name of ' Maarten Maartens ', whose tall and imposing presence I had however observed, urbane, obviously distinguished, and a little weary, as he conversed with half-closed eyes. Feeling that I was at last coming into my own, I followed dear Mrs. Gosse downstairs to a small room at the back of the house, where I found my mother sitting with the novelist and his daughter, who was beautifully dressed and—as I soon discovered—unaffectedly charming.

This epilogue to the afternoon remained in my mind as essentially harmonious and peaceful. Friendliness pervaded the room, and the pleasantly subdued light made it somehow suggestive of a Dutch painting of a family seated around a table. Dr. van der Poorten-Schwarz didn't say much, but his deep-toned deliberate voice, his stillness, and the gravely absorbent way he had of regarding those to whom he spoke—all this was expressive of the wisdom and humanity which must, I felt, assuredly be found in his novels. I was unaware that his writings also contained a good deal of pungent satire; and had I known more about mundane experience I might have surmised that he was philosophically speculating whether he would get back to his hotel in time to have a rest before dinner! Meanwhile his gaze rested a moment on some shelves filled with modern books. 'There', he reflectively informed us, 'are the authors whom our friend Gosse has discussed in his delightful critiques—and will never read again. We writers are fortunate when we find someone capable of exploring our works a second time!' This we received with respectful silence, no other comment seeming to be called for. At that point we were joined by Mr. Gosse, who exclaimed, while entering the room, that he had 'left no lately lingering guest unsped'. His movements were quick and almost youthful, and as he threw himself back in a chair he gave a deep spontaneous sigh of relief, including us all in a waggishly confiding glance through gold-rimmed spectacles. He then most gratifyingly explained me to Maarten Maartens as 'the very youngest of our unpublished poets, and a veritable centaur among them, since he bestrides his own Pegasus in hunt steeplechases'. He added—with a smile in my direction—that he had heard from my Uncle Hamo how I had returned in triumph with a silver cup slung from my saddle-bow.

Mr. Gosse now set off on quite a different tack, raising both hands in a characteristic gesture of mock consternation. 'But my dear Maarten Maartens, your diplomatic envoy—in his responses to the contemporary scene of English letters—is "of an impenetrability", as our noble Henry James would say! Of him he seemed scarcely to have heard, and even the name of Hardy evoked in him but a beautifully official blankness. I was, indeed, compelled to exert unexampled adroitness in avoiding an exposure of my distaste for the delirious productions of Miss Corelli, whom His Excellency appeared to accept as the foremost of her sex in modern fiction and "the eclipse and glory of her kind"! Oh, but you should have heard how I cooed to him, like the most propitiatory of turtle-doves!'

While he continued to divert us I felt—though out of my depth among most of his allusions—that I had really arrived at the fountain-head. Unaccustomed as I was to conversational virtuosity, it did not occur to me that such talk was an acquired artifice which had become as natural to him as his style of writing. I looked on him as a man in a state of temporary inspiration, and overheard him in a delicious ferment of unsophisticated bemusement.

But all too soon it was time for us to be departing; and no doubt Mr. Gosse had some apt and graceful periphrasis even for the calling of a cab. Dr. van der Poorten-Schwarz bestowed upon us a ceremonious bow, which I did my awkward best to imitate; Mrs. Gosse embraced my mother; and Mr. Gosse patted me out into the cool of the evening with cordial finality. While we were on our way to Charing Cross my mother exclaimed that she was so pleased I had heard dear Gosse in such good form. 'He does trifle so perfectly!' she said, adding that he'd almost made her feel as if she were back in the old days when she painted those little panel portraits of him and Nellie on a door in their first house in Delamere Terrace.

To me, however, it had been a tantalizing glimpse which made the journey back to Kent not unlike an exodus from Eden. What hope had I of ever being properly inside that privileged existence? Only by becoming something better than a nobody. I did not need to be reminded that Mr. Gosse was far too busy and famous to have time for giving more than fleeting encouragement to any but the most promising poets. One had to be a real success before he would open those doors beyond which all the gifted people were to be found in full enjoyment of one another's originality! It is possible, none the less, that I had enough self-confidence to believe that it would be only a matter of time before I stormed the heights of Hanover Terrace with a prodigious poem. As things turned out, my moderate display of talent enabled me to keep in touch with Mr. Gosse by post; but two years were to pass before I again appeared in his presence.

## VII

The unrevealed processes of memory are mysterious. Neither unconscious selection nor uncontrolled hazardry can be held responsible for one's recovery of some moment which emerges—actual as ever—in contrast to the generalized indistinctness wherefrom one elaborates the annals of personal experience. The summer of 1911 comes to life for me now in a coloured mental photograph of myself crouching on the tennis court at Weirleigh with a dandelion root between finger and thumb and a broken palette-knife of my mother's in the left hand. There is nothing remarkable in that, for I have always been an inveterate lawn-weeder, and one dandelion root is much the same as another. On this occasion, however, a voice invades the serene ruminations in which my weeding—and the stillness of a July evening—have involved me. 'The way you wriggled that root up makes me think that you ought to become rather a good workman with words.' The voice is Wirgie's; but time shuts up the scene before I can get a graphic view of her or hear how I replied.

Anyhow there she was, beside me on the lawn,

and her visit that summer happened to be a more than usually prolonged one, which lasted most of July and half-way through August. For when she had been with us two or three weeks and was just beginning to talk about going on to stay with her brother Theodore near St. Ives—he was the only near relative she had, and was the artist who had painted Mrs. Gosse's portrait years ago—just, I repeat, when I was wondering how to induce her to remain with us a bit longer, she slipped on a polished floor while playing with the white Persian kitten and damaged one of her ribs. The injury was diagnosed by our local doctor, a man of slow and dubious decisions, as 'cracked but not fractured'. She was forbidden to touch the piano, but persisted in doing so as soon as the first acute discomforts abated. On my mother remonstrating, she stopped playing for a few moments, swayed herself slightly, and then remarked, with heedful solemnity, '*I can hear it creaking*'. She was getting on for seventy now, and her Beethoven-playing had lost some of its passionate intensity. 'I'm only a worn-out old spinet,' she sighed, when I asked for the 'Waldstein' Sonata and lifted the piano-lid full up on to its peg. So I put the lid down again and persuaded her to be a harpsichord instead. This was a favourite game of ours, which was contrived by spreading a newspaper over the strings of the ' baby grand '. She would then tinkle and twangle through a Bach prelude—or the Toccata of Paradisi, which I never tired of hearing, so full of bygone summer and happiness its rippling cadences seemed. Afterwards I would remove the newspaper and request a *molto espressivo* performance of a little modern piece called ' Vesperale ', during which she would bend over the key-board with parodistically pensive head-shakes. Better still—if she were in the right mood—she would ' do Godowsky ', which was her impersonation of that eminent pianist executing a cantabile encore. This had emanated from a recital we had heard some years before. But the museful authority with which she played some romantic afterthought of Schumann was a thing which went a long way beyond travesty.

She was always at her best when with young people. Their bright hopefulness, as she said, made her feel able to be useful. With women nearer her own age she was liable to become remote and even morose. But when she stiffened and ' showed the white of her eye ', it was usually toward someone who was going in for being showily epigrammatic. Of one such lady I heard her say ' She talks much too well for me to be able to sit still and listen to her capriolings! ' Wirgie herself was a consistently unhurrying and cogitative talker—a quality which was accentuated when she was responding to the velocity and inconsequence of youth. Even her inimitable flippancies were somehow attuned to regretfulness. Vehemently alive though she was, one doesn't easily remember her as vivacious. In moments of jocosity she had a droll trick of making her voice grotesquely sepulchral. The only person with whom I can remember her being superficially sprightly was a near neighbour of ours—a middle-aged man who knew just how to ' rally ' her in the right way. His stock joke was to address her as ' Duchess ', and as the Duchess she was delightful. It made her feel quite *ancien régime*, she said; and when Mr. Vaughan—whom she called ' an agreeable rattle '—came to tea, she would tell him that she must go upstairs and put on her ear-rings, because she couldn't feel a proper duchess without her old rose-diamonds. Being a dingy duchess wasn't good enough for her, although she had once seen one at an agricultural show wearing clothes even older than her own. ' If a burglar were to nobble my ear-rings,' she remarked, ' I should be absolutely done for as a duchess.' (She was rather addicted to using the word ' nobble ' at that time.)

One cannot conclude a portrait of Wirgie with a paragraph of levities. For the essential thing in her character was its deep seriousness. Her pride often made her difficult, but it was a sign of the inflexible standard of honour which she demanded of herself and of others. Insincerities and broken promises shocked her as much as unkindness to animals—which she could never forgive. Lonely and sociable, complex and single-hearted, she came and went among her submissive friends, lighting up their lives by the imaginative vitality of her spirit.

* * *

At that time I was still a poor performer on the piano, but this had not deterred me from buying a considerable quantity of difficult music. My latest discovery had been Debussy. After hearing a group of his works at a recital, I had hastened from the Aeolian Hall to Augener's music shop resolved to carry home as much of him as I could, much excited by his delicate descriptiveness and his new and sumptuous subtleties of tone. It soon became obvious that my musicianship was inadequate to cope with his innovating harmonies, and that my unfluent fingers had a long way to travel before they acquired the ' Debussy touch '. Anyhow when Wirgie arrived at Weirleigh that summer she found a pile of Debussy on the piano, and I introduced him with an almost proprietary air. By then I had laboriously learnt by heart the *Sarabande*, and could just struggle through *Hommage à Rameau* without stopping altogether. I was also deriving exquisite sensations from the slow passages in *Clair de Lune*. She must have known more about this composer than she then divulged —she admitted that she had heard his *Pelléas et Mélisande*—but she had not attempted to play anything of his except the not very difficult *Arabesques*. 'But these are quite beyond my powers, you go-ahead young person!' she murmured, after glancing through the elegant intricacies of *L'Île Joyeuse*, *Reflets dans l'Eau*, and one or two other tantalizingly impressionistic pieces. Nevertheless she overcame her diffidence, had soon discovered that *Jardins sous la Pluie* was nothing like so impossible as it looked, and was able to saturate me with its representation of a drenching downpour in the darkness of a summer garden and its recognizable rain-drops tinkling into a cistern. Surely there was poetry for me, I thought, in this Debussy world, this mirrored existence where swaying reflections and voluptuous apostrophes were interwoven with the shimmer of sunset bells across calm waters, this land of eternal afternoon imbued with sensuous day-dreams, lulling and exquisite and vaguely regretful! Here I could absorb emotional richness unreluctantly; here was a refinement of ecstasy, conscious and controlled. ' Paragon among sybaritic serenaders,' Wirgie had dubbed the composer, in one of her Meredithian moments. She might also have told me that we learn the best of life unwillingly, acquiring wisdom unawares. But she understood me too well to say anything of the sort. She knew that my immature intelligence could perceive no more than the surface qualities of Debussy's art. I did not tell her that I had been attempting to express my enraptured response to the *Suite Bergamasque* in a richly unreal sonnet. But we several times discussed the *Suite*, and on one occasion I asserted that *Clair de Lune* was the loveliest thing Debussy had ever written. Its opening bars had indeed been haunting my head for weeks, and had given me a sort of unformulated heart-ache. Wirgie admitted its alluringly poetical atmosphere, but said that she preferred the *Passepied*, which she declared to be a finer though more conventional composition. When I asked why she admired it so much, she played half a page—with the right delicate dryness of touch—and then remarked that she liked it for its beautiful old-fashioned manners and loved it because it was so pathetic. Compared with *Clair de Lune* it sounded to me unromantic, and I couldn't make out why she thought it pathetic. I told her this, and she shut the piano with a sigh. She preferred Debussy when he was unsweetened, she said, instancing the early suite *Pour le Piano.* I can understand now, all these years afterwards, what the difference was—between her heart-ache and mine. It was the difference between the young and the old. Had she questioned me about the impression that I was deriving from *Clair de Lune*, I might have confessed to a dreamy idea of some illusionary lover among the fountains, cypresses, and statues of a moonrise-vista'd garden. The sonnet I had been meditating contained the line ' Moon of sad lutes and bitter serenade '; and it ended—rather effectively, I thought—as follows . . .

*And pale processions half in moonshine went*
*With litanies and low disconsolate hymns.*

It is therefore beyond argument that the music had merely made me indulge my periodic propensity for echoing the minor poetry of the 'Nineties.

Wirgie offered no direct explanation of her preference for the final movement of the *Suite.* But she told me—in a gravely unemphatic voice—how she had once seen ' the Paspy ' danced in an amateur revival of some Seventeenth Century Court Masque, to the music of a forgotten old French composer. The memory of it, she said, had often returned to her. Debussy's *Passepied*, with its innocent little descending melody, brought her just the same visualized emotion—of those dancers, all so young and charming and serenely serious, moving lightly to and fro in the quick minuet, as if the passing of time were nothing to them—though the latent pathos of life was calling to them all the while in the unheeding *moto perpetuo* of the gracious music. In some such words she gave me her interpretation of the half-page that she had played before she closed the piano with a sigh.

* * *

For me, piano-playing and writing poetry have always been closely connected. Most of my early verse was vague poetic feeling set to remembered music. Unintellectual melodiousness was its main characteristic. Rich harmonies and lingering sonorities induced a relaxation of the nerves, and acted on me like soothing and stimulating oxygen. The vibrations of certain chords had a physical effect which released the rather confused ideas that I was trying to express. All this, I feel sure, is nothing unusual. I have known cats and dogs who quite obviously got blissful enjoyment from being near the piano while I was luxuriating in slow and scrumptious tone-productions.

I must explain that abstract ideas are uncongenial to my mind. The sound of words has been more to me than skilful management of their meanings, and verbal exactitude was a late arrival in my literary development. I have always instinctively avoided the use of metaphors, except when they came uncalled-for. Indirect and allusive utterance has never been natural to me. I much prefer the poetry which I can visualize and feel to that which needs thinking out afterwards. My delight in a fine passage of poetry has therefore seldom been diminished by precise meanings being only half understood—or even wholly misunderstood—by me. For instance, when I was well over thirty I could still repeat to myself—

*And David's lips are lockt; but in divine*
*High-piping Péhlevi, with 'Wine! Wine! Wine!'*
*'Red Wine!'—the Nightingale sings to the Rose . . .*

without being aware that Péhlevi is not a place in Persia but (as FitzGerald explained in a note at the end of his poem) 'the old Heroic Sanskrit'. I may have dimly wondered why a Persian town should have been described as 'high-piping', but I was able to get quite a comfortable picture 'of some not unfrequented Garden-side' overtopped by the ivory-pale roofs and minarets of Péhlevi; and had I been asked why on earth FitzGerald called the place ' divine ', I should have replied that it was ' probably something to do with Mahomet having lived there for a bit '.

My edition of the *Rubá'iyàt* was without the Notes. It was a privately-printed quarto, dated 1883, which had belonged to my father. The boards of its binding were covered by a damask of faded rose-colour figured with old gold, and the queer coarse-woven paper on which it was printed contributed further to its esoteric attractiveness. From the time when I first discovered the book in my mother's studio—I must have been about eleven years old—I dreamily accepted the imagery and the stately beat of the Quatrains without bothering to think what they meant. And even in the summer of 1911, when Wirgie remarked that at my age I had no right to be so wrapped up in such a saddening poem, I could only reply that I'd ' never exactly thought about it being so sad as all that '. Although by then I knew quite a lot of it by heart, the flowing purple of Omar's and FitzGerald's philosophy had caused me no disquietude. At twenty-five, one rather enjoyed being warned that the Wine of Life was oozing drop by drop and the Leaves of Life falling one by one! It seemed that the only touch of sadness in the volume was my father's upright and angularly refined signature, written on the fly-leaf. But I had counteracted that by putting my own name underneath—with a purple-inked rubber stamp which I had used somewhat ubiquitously at one period of my boyhood.

* * *

While Wirgie was recovering from her mishap my mother found her ' a bit of a handful '.

' I've gone and put my foot in it again! ' she exclaimed when I got back one evening after being out all day playing cricket. ' I sent specially to Tunbridge Wells to get a lobster for her lunch,' she continued, ' but like an idiot I'd forgotten that crab and lobster are both of them poison to her system. When I went up to her room before tea to find out whether she could manage roast duck for dinner, she rolled her eye at me as if I were the villain in a melodrama and said she could scarcely believe it possible that after knowing her all these years I hadn't remembered that lobster mayonnaise always makes her swell up like a balloon! ' Apart from this, Wirgie's restlessness was causing my mother genuine anxiety lest the crepitant and oft listened-to rib might permanently refuse to mend. Next day, while we were still trying to think how to keep her amused, a friend of mine, who also happened to be a first-rate amateur musician, wrote suggesting that he should pay us a short visit. This was considered providential, and a telegram was dispatched, urging him to come as soon as he could. I took the precaution of not leading Wirgie to expect too much of him, so the surprise was well sprung; and toward the end of his first evening with us she enquired in a delighted undertone why I hadn't told her that he was such a brilliant pianist, adding that she couldn't understand how I'd kept such a feather in my cap up my sleeve so cleverly! She had apparently forgotten that I had mentioned him more than once in the past; but I had laid no stress on his musical gift, and she hadn't shown much curiosity when I had told her that I knew a man who spoke fifteen languages—including several Slavonic dialects. Anyhow Nevill Forbes had given us an exquisite evening of Debussy, Ravel, and Chausson; and it seemed that the longer this sort of thing continued the better it would be for all of us—Wirgie's strapped-up rib included.

My friendship with Forbes had originated with our old German governess, Fräulein Stoy, who had lived with his family before coming to us. Her success in teaching him the piano had been as complete as her failure to make any headway at all with me. In those days I used to hear a lot about the miraculous Nevill, who could learn languages as easily as pulling up radishes and at ten years old had been able to play the most difficult duets with his equally talented sister. In fact I sometimes thought of Fräulein's beloved Forbeses with positive aversion, so frequently had their virtues been held up to me as an example! In later years, however, when I got to know Nevill well, I found nothing in him to dislike and much to admire. He was so amiable and unassuming that I could almost forget how far he excelled me in everything I had tried to learn. His education had indeed been a triumphal progress. At Balliol he had romped through every examination; he had taken a Ph.D degree at Leipzig; and he now held the Professorship of Russian at Oxford. But I used to tell him that the only professorial thing about him was his spectacles. He could play any music at sight, and there seemed no limit to his willingness to perform one big work after another in powerful and sympathetic style.

'But this has been an orgy!' Wirgie exclaimed, when he had concluded his second evening recital at Weirleigh with Reger's *Variations and Fugue on a Theme by Bach*—a work which was in itself a banquet of musical rhetoric. Nevertheless the modest performer looked as fresh as when he had started. Blowing out the candles on the piano, he rubbed his spectacles, laughed in his nervously irresolute way, and began putting Albeniz, César

Franck, Scriabin, and other modern composers into a leather portfolio.

On the following day the weather was so perfect that my mother almost made up her mind to have dinner out on the lawn. On second thoughts she decided that it would make too much trouble for the servants, so we contented ourselves with coffee under the Irish yew outside the Studio, whence we watched an afterglow of sunset that seemed to be going on for ever while the twilight deepened and yet delayed and the scents of the garden were delicious in the dew-fall. It was one of those summers which one associated with people sitting out of doors after dinner—their voices murmuring on and on until it wasn't worth while to light the lamps in the drawing-room. The family of white owls, who lived in the pigeon-loft by day and sat in a row on the Studio roof at night, must have grown quite accustomed to the sound of conversation down below and the spurt of a match when someone lit a cigarette. One of those specially-remembered summers it was, from which one evolves a consistent impression of commingled human happiness, lighting its evening star above the remains of sunset as though coffee-drinking contentment could never be interrupted by dull days and head-ache-producing thunderstorms. Sitting under the Irish yew, we seemed to have forgotten that there was such a thing as the future, and the lingering afterglow was like an elegy on hours which had departed in acquiescent glory, leaving us to the starlight of our untroubled thoughts.

Meanwhile my mother had gone indoors, and I sat silent while Nevill Forbes and Wirgie discoursed in the dusk—their voices sounding not unlike a dialogue between a violin and a violoncello. The contrast in their vocal modulations was that he went along rapidly and fluently, while Wirgie was slow, self-contained and enquiring. He was like a cheerful animated Allegro, while she maintained the tempo of an unaccelerating Adagio. Listening to them as they compared their memories of foreign places which I'd only heard of by name, I wondered how either of them had ever found it worth while to converse with such a country bumpkin as myself!

It was nice, however, to feel that I'd been the means of bringing them together. Wirgie's personality had become more cosmopolitan than I'd ever known it before; phrases in French and German occurred in her talk with fine style and spontaneity, and she seemed to be hearing about everything that she most wanted to be reminded of. And he, with his twelve months spent in the musical centre of Leipzig, his highly-cultivated Russian relations, and the abundant Bayreuth experiences which he could harmonize with hers—was it to be wondered at that she found him so stimulating and delightful? I began to feel quite dispirited at never having been outside England since before I was born! I had got no farther than being bowed to by Maarten Maartens at the Gosses', while here was Nevill describing how he had visited Tolstoy, who for me was no more than a batch of translated novels in the drawing-room book-case—novels in a peculiarly unpleasant green cloth binding. Wirgie listened with the deepest interest to his lively and unpretentious account of how the famous man had insisted on his playing Mozart duets with his daughter, how Tolstoy had been wearing a peasant smock, while his wife was bejewelled in a low-necked evening gown in broad daylight, and how there had been a billiard-table littered with letters from all over the world—none of which Tolstoy would ever open, let alone read.

* * *

Next morning Nevill went away. His visit had been such a success that it left both Wirgie and myself feeling flat and unentertaining. She gave no sign of wanting to play the piano, and I didn't quite like to suggest it. On the day after his departure, after spending a long sultry afternoon reading *Anna Karenina* in the drawing-room, she looked up to remark that she had forgotten how strangely impressive it was. As I hadn't yet read it, I could only answer that I intended to have a go at it one of these days. 'You are much too young for it,' she replied, adding, in a tragic undertone, 'and I'm too old and weary to be any more use to you after such a wildly gifted musician as your friend Forbes!' I knew that it was no use arguing with her when she had turned moody. For a moment I wondered whether to pass it off with a joke or go out and have a putting-match with myself on the lower lawn. I did neither, but allowed myself to say what came most naturally into my mind, which was the simple statement that I had never enjoyed anyone's playing more than hers. She must have known that I really meant it, for she went over to the piano, just as she always did when I asked her to 'do Godowsky' for me. She played Schumann's *Warum*, and played it with a simplicity that somehow made it sound like a meditative coda to all the music she had ever given me. *Warum* . . . the very word was all her own. And more than then it seems so now, resurrecting as it does that vibrant low-pitched voice and the wistful drollery of those querying eyes.

# VIII

In the middle of December 1912 there was a spell of tempestuously wet weather. The country became waterlogged, and hunting was out of the question, since for me this meant taking my horses long distances by train. One afternoon after several days of enforced inactivity, I was staring out of a window in my upstairs room in the Studio, wondering how on earth to occupy my mind. Daylight was fading disconsolately from the dull gleams of water where the floods were out along the Weald, and the low-sagging leaden clouds looked full of rain. But surely, I thought, as I turned to the fire-lit book-shelves, there must be something which I could make myself settle down to read with wintertime contentment—something to make me forget how dumpy I'd felt lately about my own writing. For discouraged I was—my latest and most ambitious effort in verse having failed to produce the effect which I had confidently anticipated.

About three months before, I had written a grandiose *Ode for Music*. It was a hundred lines in length and I had composed it in a condition of ecstatic afflatus. I had in fact felt like an enthusiastic cathedral organist with all his swellest stops pulled out. Not wholly uninfluenced by *The Hound of Heaven*, I had climbed, taken wing, triumphed, and rejoiced in ' storms of jubilation ' and ' psalmodies of splendour '. I had overheard ' symphonies of flame ' and ' raptures of resistless lyring', and toward the end I claimed to have 'shared celestial commotion ! ' Here, at last, I thought, was my liberation from anaemic madrigals about moonlit gardens, thrummed by the lutes of ill-starred lovers. Intoxicated by my own mystical impressiveness, I dispatched the Ode forthwith to the Chiswick Press, who printed fifty copies in an austerely elegant format which caused me to feel prouder than ever of my supposed masterpiece. For me the Ode was all harmonious thunders of adoration with interludes of *vox humana* serenity and seraphic diminuendos. But for Mr. Gosse, to whom I posted the foremost copy of the fifty, it was, apparently, nothing of the kind. Two months had passed, and I had received no acknowledgement from him. And since he had found himself unable to say anything about it, I could only assume that my ' bright and passionate revelation ' had been merely inflated rhetoric, and that I had been led astray by my excessive spiritual sublimity! I had indeed more or less admitted the incommunicability of my emotions in the penultimate stanza, where I alluded to ' the overwhelming wonder of that vision which never mortal speech may now disclose '; but I had lifted the roof off again at the end of the Ode by exhorting the audience to

*Hearken to him who passes upward, crying—*
*' Be of untroubled heart and I will make you*
*Great with a faith which never shall forsake you,*
*Till out of death your soul shall rise undying '.*

But even this did not set Mr. Gosse alight as he sat in the elevated atmosphere of the Library of the Upper House. For it was the old story over again. I had tried to produce a glorious effect by exclaiming ' Gloria in excelsis ' and asking everyone to believe how wonderful I felt.

Meanwhile there I was in the silent Studio, with the last watery gleam of daylight dissolving from the Weald, while the brass candle-sticks on my bureau reflected the glow of a wood fire, and Burne-Jones's *Days of Creation* gazed aloofly over my head from their large dim photograph above the chimney-corner. And there—on one of the shelves along which my eyes indolently wandered—was Masefield's *Everlasting Mercy*, which I now pulled out, casually purposing to see whether its headlong octosyllabics were as exhilarating as they had been at a first reading. I had raced through the poem about twelve months before, and had been wildly excited by the impetus and naturalness which had made it so famous; and it had left me with an impression of vivid power and beauty. It had also, of course, been easy game for the parodists, owing to its startlingly individual idiom and occasional use of swear-words. So before I had so much as opened it, a second thought occurred to me. Why not amuse myself by scribbling a few pages of parody? I may as well say at once that the immediate result was something far beyond what I had intended. Having rapidly resolved to impersonate a Sussex farm-hand awaiting a trial for accidental homicide of the barman of the village ale-house, I began his story in crudest imitation of Masefield's manner. Stimulating my pencil with an occasional dose of *The Everlasting Mercy*, I found myself corking down the 'human document' with astonishing facility. After the first fifty lines or so, I dropped the pretence that I was improvising an exuberant skit. While continuing to burlesque Masefield for all I was worth, I was really feeling what I wrote—and doing it not only with abundant delight but a sense of descriptive energy quite unlike anything I had experienced before. I cannot claim that my Sussex yokel was undeviatingly true to life, but on the whole he was quite recognizable—except when he lapsed into a parenthetic passage of literary apostrophizing, like his prototype the poacher in Masefield's poem.

> *O clod-pole feet so blindly going,*
> *O seed that wasn't worth the sowing,*
> *O bumpkin bodies filled with hate,*
> *A-picking squabbles with your fate!*

At one point, however, where he was remembering his wife and children in the cottage which he would never see again, I found myself stopping to exclaim aloud that this really was darned good homely stuff. Never before had I been able to imbue commonplace details with warmth of poetic emotion. Wholly derivative from *The Mercy* though it remained, my narrative did at any rate express that rural Sussex which I had absorbed through following the Southdown hounds and associating with the supporters of the hunt. In other words I was at last doing what had been suggested by Wirgie in 1911—writing physically.

> I thought how in the summer weather
> When Bill and me was boys together
> We'd often come this way when trudgin'
> Out by the brooks to fish for gudgeon.
> I thought, When me and Bill are deaders
> There'll still be buttercups in medders,

And boys with penny floats and hooks
Catching fish in Laughton brooks . . .

Far into the night I kept up my spate of productiveness, and next day I went on with unabated intensity. By the evening I had finished it, and was counting the lines, which totalled just over five hundred. Reading it through again, I did not ask myself what use there could be in writing a poem so extravagantly unoriginal. Nothing mattered except the mental invigoration it had brought me. I felt that in the last twenty-four hours I had found a new pair of poetic legs, and the fact that they had been graciously presented to me by John Masefield made no difference to my sense of self-satisfaction.

* * *

It was now some two and a half years since I'd been in communication with that redoubtable journalist T. W. H. Crosland (whom, by the way, I had not seen 'in the flesh' since our interview at the offices of *The Academy*). In the spring of 1910 he had printed four of my sonnets, but shortly afterwards *The Academy* began a less lively career under different ownership and editorial control, and a couple more of my poems which Crosland had accepted were returned to me without comment. So I had lost sight of his literary activities until quite lately, when he had reappeared, this time as a publisher, under the name of John Richmond, Ltd. Having received some sort of prospectus of his new venture, which included a monthly magazine called *The Antidote*, I responded by sending Crosland a copy of my Ode. His reply arrived a day or two after my feat of Masefieldian burlesque.

DEAR SIR,

I have read with pleasure your Ode for Music. You may take it from me that it is a good piece of work, and as fine, and nobly intended, as anything we have had in this way for a long time. But it suffers from what we may call ' youngness ' and want of mellowness and beating out. (He went on to suggest several verbal emendations, which I need not reproduce.) There are other things to be said, but you are a much better poet than I am and I don't want to upset you. If you like, I will print the Ode in the next issue of my paper *The Antidote*. I can't pay you for it, because I have no money; but I can make a song about it, and you will be in good company and in the only paper which doesn't take advertisements.

Yours truly,

T. W. H. CROSLAND.

P.S. I shall be rather heart-broken if you don't let me have this Ode. So that unless there are insuperable difficulties please say the word.

The notion of there being, at that date, any insuperable difficulty connected with my permitting an editor to print one of my poems now strikes me as laughable. Nevertheless I must have replied somewhat self-disparagingly to his criticisms, for in his next letter he urges me not to be too hard on myself or take too much notice of his corrections, adding that he will be sending me a proof soon after Christmas. The Ode duly appeared in the February number, but there is no evidence that my invocation to 'angels of God and multitudes of Heaven' caused any raptures of religious feeling among those who paid their penny (that was its price) for *The Antidote*.

By then, however, I had something else to think about. In the middle of January I sent my parodistic poem to Crosland, but without any definite idea that I was offering it for publication. In fact I didn't even trouble to give it a title—merely writing 'Rigmarole' at the top of the first page of the manuscript. So I was genuinely astonished by his assumption that I wanted him to publish it. This he at once offered to do, on condition that I contributed ten pounds towards expenses. He suggested calling it *The Gentle Murderer*, by Peter Expletive, and offered to write a pseudonymous and mock-adulatory introduction. He had for some time been attacking Masefield's narrative poems with bludgeoning vindictiveness, so my parody was just what he wanted. His only objection was that it 'needed a bit more bawdry and suggestiveness'—a defect which I had no inclination, and very little ability, to repair. He must have realized that it was a hybrid production, mainly stimulated by admiration for its model; but there seemed to be no point in my telling him that it had been written with no active intention of diminishing Masefield's reputation as a poet. I knew nothing of him personally except that he had been a sailor. Anyhow he was far-off and famous, and the authorship was to be kept a dead secret. (I have good reason for believing that Crosland allowed it to be assumed that he had written it himself.) Before long I was having a glorious time with my very first set of galley-proofs, verbally strengthened in a few places by Crosland, who was giving me a good lesson in the elimination of unconvincing epithets. By now I was so fond of the poem that I knew it almost by heart! The title was to be *The Daffodil Murderer* by Saul Kain—Masefield's latest poem being *The Daffodil Fields*—and the facetious preface laid stress on the author having been a soldier who had 'fought for his country on many a bloody field' but was 'fonder of poetry than pipe-clay'—words which afterwards achieved an almost prophetic accuracy. Opposite the title-page I put a quotation from Chaucer which by 'beginner's luck' I discovered in the first few minutes of searching for an equivalent to the lines by Lydgate that were the epigraph of *The Everlasting Mercy*.

> '*As best I may I will my woe endure,*
> *Nor make no countenance of heaviness.*'

Thus the whole thing was 'determined, dared, and done' within three weeks of my sending it to John Richmond, Ltd., and on February 10th I awoke as the anonymous author of a sixpenny pamphlet in a cheerful orange-coloured wrapper. Nor, I imagine, was any heaviness observable in my countenance on that eventful day. Referring to my hunting diary, I find that I was out with the Southdown hounds, who met at 'The Six Bells, Chailey', and killed their fox at five-thirty after a tremendous woodland hunt. 'The going', I noted, was 'terrible sticky'.

* * *

A thousand copies of *The Daffodil Murderer* were printed, and Crosland held out hopes that 'we might be able to get rid of a couple of thousand more if it caught on'. By our epistolary agreement he was to pay me twopence on each copy sold; but my *Academy* experience of his non-payment of guineas for poems seemed a guarantee that I should never see any of my ten pounds again, whatever else might happen! There was however a faint chance that my pamphlet might 'catch on', and I now bethought me how I could make an independent effort to increase the sales. The only person I could think of as likely to be helpful was Mr. Bowes, the Cambridge bookseller, in the shades of whose agreeable shop I had overspent my allowance so rewardingly when I was an undergraduate. So to him I wrote, politely drawing his attention to my sixpennyworth. In a subsequent daydream it was just possible to imagine the fame of the slim yellow volume spreading like wild-fire among the lively-minded young men of the University, while Bowes & Bowes urgently ordered more and more copies from Crosland's office in Conduit Street, where his opinion of my business ability would go up by leaps and bounds. Everyone in Cambridge would be asking who 'Saul Kain' really was—and I shouldn't have the smallest objection to their knowing. . . . Sitting at his desk in the far corner of the shop, little Mr. Bowes would watch one of his assistants putting another pyramid of *Daffodil Murderers* on a table, and would murmur to his ink-stand and ledger that there hadn't been such a success since—here my inventiveness failed me, for the only name I could think of was *The Everlasting Mercy*, which was obviously inappropriate—*Rejected Addresses* was the sort of thing I needed, but that had been about a hundred years ago. . . . ' Dear me,' Mr. Bowes would gently observe to the Provost of King's or someone like that who had just arrived to secure another dozen copies of the fifth edition, ' it seems only yesterday that young Mr. Sassoon used to look in on his way back from lectures to choose a morocco binding for one of his favourite poets. He went down without taking a degree, I think; but I always felt sure that we should hear of him again '. ' Ah well, Mr. Bowes,' the Provost would reply, ' your anticipation has been abundantly fulfilled. *The Daffodil Murderer* is a work which merits the widest attention and cannot be too strongly recommended to all lovers of good literature '. (This was my idea of what the reviewers ought to say about it.) But as a matter of fact the only result of my sales-stimulating effort was an angry letter from Crosland, who informed me that ' Messrs. Bowers and Bowers of Cambridge ' (when he wanted to be rude he always spelt people's names wrongly) had written ordering twelve copies of ' Mr. Sassoon's parody '.

He reprimanded me severely for divulging the authorship, and asserted that success depended on it remaining unknown. He would be glad if in future I would be good enough to refrain from doing this sort of thing. As a sign of his disapproval his letter was typewritten, and it wouldn't have surprised me if his secretary had been instructed to spell my name Sasson! I felt a little hurt and annoyed; but that sort of collision was to be expected when dealing with a rough customer like Crosland.

In the meantime I had sent a copy to Mr. Gosse, and by a charming coincidence his reply reached me on St. Valentine's Day.

My dear Siegfried,

*The Daffodil Murderer* is a composition which interests me very much, and about which I feel a difficulty in defining my opinion. It is a very clever, brilliant thing, and displays powers which I had not expected from you. But, apart from the ' Preface ', which is a very amusing (and well-deserved) bit of satire, what puzzles me about the poem is that it is not really a parody at all. It is a pastiche. It treats a Masefield subject exactly in Masefield's own manner, as if you had actually got into Masefield's own skin, and spoke with his voice. There is nothing comic about it. A tale of rustic tragedy is told with real pathos and power, only—exactly as Masefield would tell it. The end is extremely beautiful.

I have given a copy of the D.M. to Mr. Edward Marsh, who is the choragus of the new poets, and has published the interesting anthology of *Georgian Poetry* which I daresay you have seen. Mr. Marsh is most curious to see what else you have written, and I should like you to make up a parcel of your pamphlets, and send them to him. I should like you to get into friendly relations with Mr. Marsh, who is a most charming man, extremely interested in poetry, and the personal friend of all the new poets. It would be useful to you, I think, as you lead so isolated a life, to get into relations with these people, who are of all schools, but represent what is most vivid in the latest poetical writing. Let me know what you think of this suggestion. It is time, I think, for you to begin to tilt up the bushel under which your light has hitherto been burning.

Yours very sincerely,

EDMUND GOSSE.

It is no exaggeration to say that I read this letter with a sort of blissful stupefaction. But it would be transparently untruthful to claim that my immediate afterthoughts were exclusively bemused by child-like gratification. No; I realized quite clearly that—as I may have expressed it to myself—' the good old *Daffodil Murderer* had jolly well done the trick for me with the literary nuts at last '. There was no nonsense about Mr. Gosse's letter, which was evidently intended to show that he no longer doubted my ability to become an effective writer. Receiving it in the same spirit, I returned his glossy House of Lords notepaper to its envelope with the sober respect that such a remunerative document deserved, took a deep breath of air which symbolized the elixir of success, and then sauntered across to the Studio to make up a parcel of my pamphlets for Mr. Marsh.

Of him I had hitherto known nothing at all. Nor had I yet seen the *Georgian Poetry* anthology, though I had been meaning to buy it. The fact that Mr. Gosse had referred to him as a ' choragus' dimly suggested the leader of the chorus of elders in a Greek play, so I now visualized him as a semi-venerable Aristarchus with a stylish silvery beard. In giving me his address Mr. Gosse had appended C.M.G. to his name, which, of course, added considerably to his impressiveness. Anyhow there could be no doubt that he was the very man for me—as he had already been for the poets who were in his anthology, which was already becoming quite famous. While bemedalling my neat package with scarlet sealing-wax, I probably said to myself that old Crosland could ruddy well go and put his head in a bag. For it really was a relief to feel that I had outsoared the shadow of his Grub Street brawlings. The February *Antidote* had contained a quite repulsively rude free-verse satire about Masefield, and it was obvious that in Crosland I had acquired a 'choragus' whom Mr. Gosse could under no circumstances describe as 'charming'!

Meanwhile I was beginning to keep a sharp look out for Press notices of the *Murderer*. Nothing happened until the end of the second week. How well I remember reading my first review! I had been hunting with the Southdown on a Saturday, and was taking the familiar evening train home from Lewes to Tunbridge Wells. At the book-stall I bought all the likely periodicals, waited until the train was under way, lit my pipe, and then settled down to 'see whether there was anything about me' in *The Spectator*, *Saturday Review*, *Athenæum*, and one or two other weekly journals. I drew all the coverts blank—all except one! *The Athenæum* did indeed give tongue about my performance, and here is what it said. 'This is a pointless and weak-kneed imitation of *The Everlasting Mercy*. The only conclusion we obtain from its perusal is that it is easy to write worse than Mr. Masefield.'

That was all. The only conclusion I 'obtained' from its perusal was that it was difficult to imagine a young writer receiving a more unmerciful first review of his first published work. And the only comment I could make on it was the school-boy phrase—'absolutely putrid!' My disappointment would however have been mitigated had I been aware that Crosland was a bitter enemy of *The Athenæum*, which had evidently assumed him to be the author of the *Murderer*, and had welcomed the opportunity of landing him one on the jaw.

I don't suppose that the spiteful paragraph interfered with my night's rest for many minutes, but if it did I received full compensation on Monday morning in the form of a long letter from Mr. Marsh. Much to my surprise, the editor of *Georgian Poetry* began by saying that he knew no reason why I should care tuppence what he thought of my poems; he was sending his criticisms for what they were worth, and if I didn't want them I must put the blame on Mr. Gosse (who would probably have exclaimed 'Fiddlesticks!' both to Mr. Marsh and myself). His letter consisted of a detailed analysis of my sonnets and lyrics. Of *The Daffodil Murderer* he merely remarked that it was good, but that he couldn't make out whether it was a parody or an imitation.

The ensuing quotation will show that he put

his finger on all the weaknesses in my work, while according it much generous appreciation.

'I think it certain that you have a lovely instrument to play upon and no end of beautiful tunes in your head, but that sometimes you write them down without getting enough meaning into them to satisfy the mind. Sometimes the poems are like pearls, with enough grit in the middle to make the nucleus of a durable work, but too often they are merely beautiful soap-bubbles which burst as soon as one has had time to admire the colours. I believe there is a good as well as a bad sense in which there must be fashions in poetry, and that a vein may be worked out, if only for a time. The vague iridescent ethereal kind had a long intermittent innings all through the nineteenth century, especially at the end, and Rossetti, Swinburne, and Dowson could do things which it is no use trying now. It seems a necessity now to write either with one's eye on an object or with one's mind at grips with a more or less definite idea. Quite a slight one will suffice. To take some examples from your work: "Morning Land" means that old English songs are like the dawn—"Arcady Unheeding" that country folk don't pay attention to the beauties of nature—and "Dryads" that the open country gets light earlier than the woods. These are small simple points, slightly treated; but they are enough to keep the tunes from cloying, and the result is to my mind real beauty (especially in " Dryads ", which I think exquisite). On the other hand " Processions " and " Ambassadors " seem to me almost meaningless.'

Mr. Marsh went on to remind me, very pertinently, that my sonnets contained far too much of the worn-out stuff and garb of poetry, instancing our old friend ' Passion with poisonous blossoms in her hair ', ' Dungeons of dim sighing ', ' Frantic waifs of plague and sin from direful cities ', and other absurdities. The sonnet he liked best was *Goblin Revel*, which was, he said, exactly like the dance of grotesques in the Russian ballet *Oiseau de feu*. Had I seen it? he asked—in his unawareness that I had yet to discover the Russian Ballet. Anyhow his little essay on my poetical works gave me deep satisfaction, as well it might; and he concluded by asking me to come and see him in London. It seemed that I had found someone who could help me not only to ' tilt up the bushel under which my light had been burning ' but also to achieve a less outmoded manner of writing.

## IX

There are moments when the technique of artfully-contrived autobiography becomes difficult to sustain—when the task of keeping the sprawled untidiness of the past inside the frame of a discreet literary method makes one long to launch out into loquacity with an easy assumption that one is addressing somebody who doesn't need quite so much explanatory assistance. In such a mood one is liable also to lose patience with one's ' dear departed ' self. Why *can't* he hurry up and get rid of all that preposterous youngness? one exclaims, while watching him begin yet another self-engrossed little journey toward nothing in particular. One watches and reflects—but how rarely one catches a really convincing view of the unglazed and unvarnished blunderer that he was! Meanwhile the inexorable rules of slow-motion reminiscence must be obeyed; the mirror must be kept polished, each pictured episode carefully composed, and all youth's gesticulating volubility and convulsiveness taken for granted or toned down to a harmonious retrospect. Unfussed as ever, the autumnal autobiographer continues.

In March, 1913, there were two 'little journeys' which cannot be left unchronicled. I must add that neither of them led 'toward nothing in particular', since one of them took me to a first meeting with my old friend Sir Edward Marsh, and the other to my first private conversation with my old friend Sir Edmund Gosse. But here again I am dependent on that undiscerning self of mine, when I would much prefer to know and narrate exactly what my two old friends said about him next time they met. 'Curiously rudimental and inarticulate', Gosse may have remarked, adding—with a gleam of his eminent archness—'But few of us, my dear Eddie, have been altogether exempt from those disabilities in our earlier years. Be kind to him, therefore, and the lips of his Muse may yet be unlockt to amaze us!'

There is no occasion for me to wax conjectural about the effect I had made on 'my dear Eddie' when lunching with him at the National Club in Whitehall. I seem to remember that he accepted my conversational incoherence with graceful adroitness; and I am certain that by the time I had 'put myself outside' a plate of the steak-and-kidney pudding which he had confidently recommended I was no longer able to think of him as 'Mr. Marsh'. For although over forty he was surprisingly youthful in appearance, and the silver-bearded Aristarchus whom I had imagined might, with qualifications, have been described as a monocled young man of fashion—among the qualifications being a suggestion of political affinities in the eye-brows (he had for a time been private secretary to Joseph Chamberlain). There I was, anyhow, in a highly civilized Club overlooking a pleasant garden, blurting out my ideas on poetry to a delightful C.M.G. who insisted on behaving as though I were his equal. After lunch my condition of gauche gratification reached a climax.

While sipping our coffee we were joined by Austin Dobson, whose works I had known with affection ever since I was old enough to appreciate verse at all. He was very gentle and unassertive, but, as was only right and proper, I listened with unrelaxing deference to the little that he found to say. I can remember only a single utterance of his quiet and deliberate voice, which happened to be his parting remark in the hall of the Club when we were about to go our separate ways. 'We are all waiting for Mr. Marsh to give us a volume of his own verses.' (A diffident murmur of dissent from Mr. Marsh gave no hint that he would some day earn the laurel as an ideal translator of La Fontaine and Horace.) I wish now that I had been impulsive enough to tell the modest old poet how, at a very tender age, I had saved up my shillings to buy his Collected Poems—in full polished tree-calf—from the Army and Navy Stores—as a birthday present for my mother, who was as fond of his writings as I was. I wish, too, that I could have told him that his delicious verses had been my earliest model when attempting to write with delicacy and precision. But such revelations only become possible when one is old enough to view the past in perspective and proportion.

My recollections of visiting Mr. Gosse at the House of Lords are somewhat hazy, for I was too shy to be able to register such impressions as I received. I went there one afternoon at his bidding, and was led to the Library, where he made gracious efforts to put me at my ease. It was not surprising, however, that I felt, as it were, mentally muted; my breath was bated and my tongue moved on tip-toe. I was over-awed by the conjunction of Mr. Gosse—with whom I was alone for the first time—and such august surroundings; in fact it was much the same as if 'Mr. Marsh' had invited me to lunch with him at Buckingham Palace. Absurd enough it seems now, since that beautiful Library was surely an ideal background for the Edmund Gosse of my imaginations.

It was a good example of the incongruous way

things happen, especially in one's youth. I had spent more time thinking well of Mr. Gosse than of any other living writer. He had befriended and encouraged me, and I deeply desired to be at my best with him. Yet here I was, awkward and tongue-tied, and all the time in danger of saying something inept or even rude. The last thing in the world I wanted was to 'go red in the face' and make stupid remarks. But I had already done so once, when he asked me—with a straight look and in a guarded tone of voice—'What kind of a person is this Crosland, with whom you have recently been associated?' His question had taken me by surprise, for it had been delivered without any preliminaries. But why—I asked myself afterwards—why had I been able to utter no better reply than a clumsily-mumbled 'Oh, he's not a bad sort of chap', without even explaining that the only time I'd seen him had been nearly four years ago, apart from the fact that I'd often suspected that he wasn't a 'good chap' at all! 'Indeed! What I myself have heard of him has been altogether to the contrary', was Mr. Gosse's only rejoinder. And I do not doubt that, had he chosen to be candid, he could have told me a great deal about Crosland's chequered career!

Reverting to his previous urbanity, he now conducted me along a series of privilege-imbued passages until we arrived at a stately doorway through which he allowed me, with a finger to his lips, to take a peep at their Lordships themselves, engaged in actual Debate. Solemnly I gazed at the dim-lit, rich, and lofty interior, and for a while we overheard the level drone of a remotely speechifying peer. Becoming my unaffected self, I spontaneously remarked—in a respectful undertone—'Anyone would almost think they were all half asleep!' For the scene did somehow suggest a dream-like and drowsy magnificence, as though the Lords were conferring on affairs of State in an endless afternoon which existed apart from the workaday world. My artless comment appeared to gratify Mr. Gosse, who murmured—with a smile that was almost fraternal—'Some of them, I doubt not, are indulging in a decorous doze. The speaker is one of the most profusely unenlivening of our hereditary legislators!'

After this little incident I went away feeling that there was some hope, at any rate, of Mr. Gosse wishing to see me again.

* * *

For the next few weeks I was very much absorbed by the urgent business of riding in point-to-point races. Strictly speaking, these events have no claim to be dwelt on, since this narrative professes to be about my career as a poet, and I have already given my horse Cockbird a copious chapter to himself. For the sake of contrast, however, I will supplement the self-portrait with a couple of snap-shots of myself as a race-rider—at the same time confessing that such open-air memories make easier and more enjoyable recording than my activities as a man of letters.

Putting up my mental field-glasses, therefore, I focus them on the finish of the Heavy Weight Race at the Southdown Meeting. Here comes Cockbird, striding collectedly toward the penultimate stake-and-binder, with another competitor alongside of him and all the others far behind. But I am in the saddle now—the mental field-glasses discarded—and as we land over the fence I feel one of the stirrup-leathers snap, and put a hand down to rescue it from falling, though why I should be bothering about saving a stirrup-iron at such a critical moment I really don't know! But the Gunner Major beside me appears to be in trouble with his mount, and I feel full of confidence. Sure enough, after flying the last fence Cockbird keeps up a good enough pace to win comfortably by a couple of lengths. Returning to my role of spectator I watch myself passing the

Judge's waggon. Finishing in nice quiet style, one hopes—hands well down and eyes looking straight ahead. Not a bit of it! The successful rider is actually waving the stirrup-iron above his head and grinning exultantly at the Judge—a genial and popular ex-Master of the Hounds. Not what I ought to have been doing, of course, but how revealingly characteristic!

The second snap-shot shows me contesting a similar finish at the Mid-Kent Stag Hounds Meeting a fortnight later. There were nine runners, but two of them are more than a field ahead of the rest, and one of the two is Cockbird. The other—ridden by a man I cordially dislike—has been pulling hard all the way and is still going strong. But he is a sketchy jumper, and the third fence from the end is a rather stiff one. He 'takes it at the roots', and I look back to see them both rolling on the ground. I finished alone—this time with complete decorum. It was one of the best moments in my sporting career; but the significant part of the anecdote remains to be told. After weighing-in, I felt that my excitement must be controlled, so instead of watching the next race I wandered off to think things over by myself. I knew that I had ridden with more judgement than on previous occasions, but I hadn't been expecting to win, so I was wildly elated, and afraid of showing it too much among my congratulatory friends. Leaning my elbows on a five-barred gate, I stared unseeingly across the Weald while the distant bawlings of the bookmakers gradually subsided. After an interval of almost unnatural silence—during which I vaguely realized that it was a great relief to be away from it all—a renewed outburst of cheers and shoutings told me that the Open Race had duly arrived at its result. It was now that my cooled-down brain was struck by the thought that my own win had been superseded by someone else's. Not a very profound or difficult idea to be struck by—but it is the first instance I can remember of a detached sense of proportion about my doings in relation to life as a whole. Anyhow I got as far as admitting that I'd exaggerated my own importance as a participator in the Mid-Kent Staghounds Point-to-point Races at Sutton Valence in A.D. 1913!

Not many days after my second winning ride I received a letter from Crosland in which, undiscouraged by the failure of *The Daffodil Murderer* to sell more than a few hundred copies, he asked to be allowed to publish a small volume of my poems. This I decided not to do, partly because so few of them seemed good enough, but mainly owing to Eddie Marsh having warned me that my methods were a bit behind the times. Crosland, on the other hand, had always accepted my cliché phrases with unconcern. He had no use at all for the poets of the Georgian anthology, which he must have read with blind intolerance—if he read it at all. His modernism had stopped short at W. E. Henley, the restrained irregularities of whose later verse experiments he loosely imitated. He was Henley's disciple in his trenchant journalism, and also in his personal poetic attitude, which was that of a man whose head was bloody but unbowed. But when Henley wrote 'Out of the night that covers me' he had been badly bludgeoned by fate. Crosland could claim no more than that he was a tough antagonist who looked for trouble wherever he could find it Meanwhile I offered him—on the spur of the moment—my five-year-old fantasia *Orpheus in Diloeryum*, since it seemed a pity to lose a chance of publishing something, especially after being told by Mr. Gosse that the time had come for me to stop hiding my light under a bushel. Crosland consented, rather unenthusiastically, on condition that I contributed ten pounds toward expenses, and I determined to wait until I saw it in proof-sheets and then make as many alterations as possible.

One morning shortly after this, I called by appointment at the office of John Richmond Ltd., which was immediately above the Rolls-Royce show-rooms in Conduit Street. That problematically ' good chap ' Crosland received me with brusque geniality, but my book needed very little discussing. He inquired whether he should send me a set of ' galleys ' or put it straight into paged proofs. Unaware that it made any difference to the printer, I chose the latter. In paged proofs, I felt, it would look nicer and be easier to revise. Crosland then invited me to ' come and have some lunch at the place across the road ', but I had already arranged to go somewhere else. The place he referred to must have been the Café Royal, a resort of his—unknown to me at that time—where, I have since heard, he was in the habit of asking everyone he met to lend him half-a-crown. Nobody minded having half-a-crown borrowed off him, he is reputed to have remarked.

I had withheld from him my opinion that *Orpheus in Diloeryum* needed a good deal of overhauling, but when the proofs arrived I happened to be in exactly the right mood, and was delighted to find that I was seeing it with new eyes. Long passages were unhesitatingly eliminated and re-written, one improvement led to another, my inventiveness increased through what it fed on, and by the time I'd finished the job every page was an arabesque of interpolations. I couldn't help thinking that when Crosland saw those sheets he could hardly fail to recognize that they represented an impressive ebullition of unfettered inspiration. I was therefore completely taken by surprise when the proofs evoked a letter of indignant protest, coupled with a demand for another ten pounds. He asserted that the type-setting would have to be done practically all over again. In this he was, of course, fully justified, but I had no knowledge of the expensiveness of re-setting page proofs, so I assumed that he was 'trying to do me in the eye' and left his letter unanswered. I had never really wanted *Orpheus* to be the first of my works to appear with my name attached to it, so I now persuaded myself that I was well out of it.

A few months later I made an attempt to recover the proofs, for the sake of my revisions. But by then the owner of John Richmond Ltd. had compulsively got rid of Crosland, who wrote me a very decent letter in which he seemed genuinely concerned about the proofs, which had disappeared, no-one knew where. The new manager repudiated all responsibility for the publication of poor *Orpheus*; so all that I had to show for it was my uncorrected duplicate copy. This still exists, neatly bound in half-vellum, but whether it is entitled to call itself a first edition I do not know.

# X

During the summer of 1913 my mind was much occupied with anticipations of next hunting season. For it had been arranged that I was going to live in Warwickshire for six months, taking four horses with me. The way all this came about has been narrated in the memoirs of Sherston, to which I must refer the reader, who can therefore regard this chapter as an unavoidable supplement that does its best to avoid repetition.

I had often thought that if ever I came into a fortune I would go off and hunt in the Shires, so my ambition was to some extent being achieved. The qualifying elements were that the Atherstone hunt was only on the borders of the real grass countries, and that my means were barely adequate for the enterprise. Anyhow this was to be the climax of my sporting career; and there were many portentous discussions with my groom and mentor Richardson, for whom the Weald of Kent was a somewhat penitential region to live in from the point of view of hunting facilities.

About the middle of September I arrived at the village of Witherley to join my friend Norman Loder, who was starting his first season as

Master of the Atherstone, hunting the hounds himself four days a week. Richardson was to follow me with the horses about a month later. Norman had taken a moderate-sized house quite near the Kennels, but it would not be ready to move into for several weeks. Since the beginning of May he had been living in the huntsman's cottage, and his habits were so simple that, had he been alone, I think he would have preferred to remain there.

I suppose that I must have enjoyed my Atherstone season most when regular hunting was in full swing and I had got to feel at home in the new surroundings. But my kindliest requickening of memory belongs to those first weeks, when everything was being intensely experienced and Norman and I were living in three small rooms, just as we did when I used to stay with him down in Sussex at the Southdown Kennels and treadle out the '*New World*' *Symphony* on the pianola in the evenings, or play '*Down in the Forest*' on the wheezy little gramophone while he fell asleep in his arm-chair.

I asked nothing better, for the time being, than those five mornings a week cub-hunting, when we got up before it was light, swallowed a cup of cocoa and a boiled egg, and trotted away in the misty-smelling September daybreak to draw some locally-renowned covert where—as Norman had probably remarked—'foxes were terrible plentiful and needed thinning out and giving some exercise'. I would be on one of his new horses, with strict orders not to knock its legs about on the hard ground or lark it over timber; and though the horses usually gave me an uncomfortable ride to the meet, I was making mental notes of the country all the time and loving every minute of it as I jogged along with the hunt second-horsemen, one of whom carried a leather bag from which protruded the complacent but inquiring head of a terrier. At the meet there would be less than a dozen riders, and a delightful feeling of the world being only half-awake. And very soon I should find myself posted at the far corner of—was it Twycross Wood?—after being warned not to let any of the cubs get across the lane into Gopsall deer-park.

Seeing it all again so clearly, I can almost re-smell the early autumn air, while the musical cry of hounds goes swinging round the covert and the voices of the hunt-servants are heard with 'Tallyo bike' and other cub-scaring exhortations, varied by saddle-rappings and rebukes of 'Ware rabbit' to members of the young entry. An indignant cock-pheasant whirrs upward from the undergrowth and skims away across a stubble field. A hound lollops past me and plunges through the brambly hedge into the wood, while I wonder how long it will take me to learn all their names—a feat which I had more or less mastered with the Southdown. . . . Had I been more of an adept in physical sensations, I should have been conscious that in such mornings there was the joy of something done for the first time, something which returns to one's mind long afterwards with constant insistence on the warmth and radiance of its irrevocable reality. But youth excels in unawareness. Least of all does it know how the artist memory will bring it back to life. Forgetful of the pen between his fingers, forehead on hand, middle-age looks back across the years, while the clock ticks unheeded on the shelf, and the purring flames of the fire consume the crumbling log.

There was indeed something almost idyllic about those first weeks, though no-one could have been more matter-of-fact than Norman in his way of doing things. The countryside was still in its summer green, and the afternoon roads hot and dusty. We went about the country calling on helpful farmers and conferring with untalkative keepers about the supply of foxes in woods which also contained patrician pheasants. There was a purposeful simplicity about it all, and I had a comfortable feeling of being almost a member of the hunt establishment. It was only a prelude to the important part of the season; but the prospect of becoming socially involved in a crowd of swell hunting people caused me some trepidation, and I almost wished that the Atherstone were a country where not many came out—instead of there being anything from a hundred and fifty to three hundred at the good meets. The Atherstonians were said to pride themselves on being quite like a family party, compared with the smart hunts in the 'Shires. But they were a much larger family—though just as friendly, as I afterwards discovered—than the quiet provincial people in the South-down country, which I had found positively homely, though it wasn't a patch on the Atherstone to ride over. A fair proportion of the latter was a thruster's paradise of neat jumpable fences and well-drained grass, but the evil element in this paradise was, of course, barbed wire; and many of our expeditions included persuasive but seldom availing efforts by Norman to induce the farmers to take it down during the winter. The farmer's reply was almost always the same. He was willing to have the wire well marked with red boards, but nothing else kept the cattle in, and the ruck of the hunt knocked holes in the fences that you could drive a cart through. Such interviews usually ended with our being offered a strong dose of whisky and water. Refusal might have caused offence, so I sometimes managed to dispose of mine by pouring it surreptitiously into the pot of some ornamental plant, and more than one aspidistra had me to thank for alcoholic refreshment on a warm afternoon. Norman used to take a few sips and then hold the tumbler in his hand, adroitly discarding it at the moment of departure while telling the farmer that it was terrible kind of him to do what he could about the wire. And away we buzzed in the hard-worked old Daimler, to undergo a similar experience a few miles further on.

While going about with him I was conscious of being little more than an imitative appurtenance. In fact I could almost compare myself to the middle-aged Aberdeen terrier who invariably accompanied us. He, by the way, did his motoring in a hamper with the lid down. This was to prevent him going along with his head out of the car all the time, a habit which was considered injurious to his eye-sight. So when we started Paddy hopped into his hamper, and I arranged myself obediently in the front seat. Norman seldom deigned to tell me where we were going, since he preferred not to give himself trouble with explanations. While we drove along the attractively tortuous by-roads I would sometimes venture a question, but his replies were blunt though sufficient.

'Who lives in there, Norman?' I once inquired, as we passed some park gates and an imposing avenue.

'Hopping lame with gout and doesn't give a bean to the Hunt,' was the answer, disregarding the owner's name.

Now and again he would volunteer a comment of his own. For instance, after skirting a straggling and ill-favoured town which was, I had gathered, mainly addicted to the manufacture of boots, he suddenly exclaimed—

'They never ought to have built a place like that so near Burbage Wood!'

I also remember how—while we were gravely inspecting the main earths in a large and well-stocked covert near Market Bosworth—I ejaculated, in a moment of mental elevation, 'Just fancy the Battle of Bosworth Field having happened only just outside here!'

He merely stared at me with—as we used to say—a face like a boot. Then, after relighting his pipe, he gazed gloomily at the cavernous entrances to the fox-earth and made the following rejoinder:—

'It absolutely defeats me, Sig, how we're ever going to get this place properly stopped till we've got rid of all the badgers.'

He had no time to waste on flights of fancy about whatever might have happened in the scenery outside Sutton Ambion Wood four hundred years before he was born.

Mind-sight recovers the pair of us as we emerge from the wood and cross the rushy pasture land of Bosworth Field with the sedate old Aberdeen at our heels. There is Norman, tall and limber-built, with his neatly-gaitered legs and deliberate way of walking, his brown felt hat tilted over his eyes, and a long-stemmed pipe between his teeth. And there am I, much the same height, adapting my pace to his, and thinking how pretty Stoke Golding church looks on its low green hill with evening sun-rays touching the spire and lighting up the windows of the clustering village. As we get into the car Norman remarks that 'the crab of Sutton Ambion is the canal'. Indicating the direction of the water-way with his pipe-stem, he explains that the foxes nearly always run that side and spoil a good hunt. He adds that 'this part of the country is simply lousy with hares'.

Thuswise he used to provide an antidote to my poetical-mindedness and indulgence in dreamy sensibility. He knew that in most ways we were totally unlike, and was only dimly aware of my literary ambitions. If I hadn't been keen on golf and hunting our friendship could never have existed. On that basis he accepted me for what I was, just as I accepted him. He was one of those people whose strength is in their consistent simplicity and directness, and who send out natural wisdom through their mental limitations and avoidance of nimble ideas. Such characters cannot be epitomized in phrases. They are positive in their qualities and actions, getting things done instead of stopping to ask why they are doing them. He was kind, decent, and thorough, never aiming at anything beyond plain common-sense and practical ability. Tolerant and reliable, he taught me to associate easily with a varied assortment of human types. Everything that I learnt from his example was to my lasting advantage, and the amount he contributed to the Sherstonian side of my personality was incalculable.

★ ★ ★

In due course we transferred ourselves from the cottage at the Kennels to Witherley Lodge, which was only a few hundred yards along the lane, and could be described as a compact and moderately commodious red brick residence, standing a little way back from the Watling Street in a small garden that had no apparent intention of growing anything except a few evergreens and two or three charmless trees. In other words it was utilitarian rather than attractive, both inside and out.

We were now joined by an Eton contemporary of Norman's named Charles Wiggin, who shared a stable with me. We also shared the services of a young man who cleaned our hunting clothes, so for the first time in my life I could claim that I had half a valet. When Norman laconically announced that Wiggin was coming, I couldn't help wondering how well I should get on with him, since I had no idea what he was like. I need not have worried, for it was obvious from the first that he was one of the nicest people I had ever known, unfailingly good-humoured and companionable. The only complaint he made about anything was that he was compelled to miss one day's hunting a week. The reason for this was that duty called him three days a week to Birmingham, where he attended at the office of his father's business, which was concerned with the manufacture of Nickel. For this ductile metal I never heard him express any enthusiasm, though I gathered that it had made the fortune of his family. So it did not surprise me when I heard, a few years later, that he had severed his connexion with Nickel to become a successful M.F.H., having in the meantime taken part in the Battle of Beersheba and been promoted to the command of the Staffordshire Yeomanry.

Charles had already hunted a good deal with the Atherstone, so he was able to introduce me to everyone and tell me all about them. The Atherstonians were a source of continual amusement to him. He liked them—he never willingly disliked anyone—but the oddities and idiosyncrasies of some of them afforded ample material for facetious description and good-natured anecdote. One of his stock jokes was ' Master, I want to introduce you to my boy ', which had originated from a septuagenarian landowner who rode up to Norman at a meet with a red-coated gentleman beside him who looked to be well over forty. In fact he supplied our evenings with just what was needed in the way of social enlivenment, for Norman and I were apt to be a bit prosy about the day's sport when we were alone, though he liked to be told what ' the field ' had been doing and saying while he was hunting hounds—which he did in a state of mental detachment that made him oblivious to everything else.

On the first Monday in November we successfully put the anxieties of the opening meet behind us. It was bright dry weather and no one expected scent to be more than moderate, but Norman added to the good opinions he had already won by his imperturbable handling of the hounds and the quietly capable way in which he kept with them all the time. ' He goes over the country as if it wasn't there,' one of the sagest subscribers remarked in my hearing. And this was true enough, for he never seemed to have more than half his mind on the fences he was jumping, and made every horse look like a safe conveyance. Thereafter the weeks slipped away very quickly, while bad scenting days became more infrequent and people gave up grumbling—as they always do—that they'd never known the ditches so blind as they were this season. Hunting continued uninterrupted by hard weather, and I have always considered it providential that my most ambitious season was so kind to me with its climate. Looking through the tersely technical entries in my diary, I find that during the whole of that winter we were only stopped three days by frost.

That diary of mine is a tantalizingly undiscursive document for my present purpose. Most of it might have been written by Norman himself, who kept a more exactly detailed but similarly laconic log-book of each day's sport. The outline of what we did is there, but most of the things which would now interest me are omitted, as the following examples will show.

*November* 14. *Broughton Astley*. Found in a hedge close to Dunton Osiers and ran well for over thirty minutes to Kilworth Sticks (Pytchley covert). Five-mile point. Several fresh foxes there; got one away but he got to ground a short distance from the covert. A very nice hunt over a fine line of country. Rode Crusader. Fell once. Found a brace in Sander's Kale field at Gilmorton and hunted one a short distance when he got in under a rick. Bolted him and had a slow hunt round Gilmorton. Drew Bitteswell blank. Scent poor in the afternoon. Rode Cockbird second. Home seven o'clock.

*December* 3. *Elford*. Found Haselour and ran across the river into the Meynell country, through Catton Park (twenty minutes to there, very fast, but we had to go round to a bridge and hardly saw them at all). From there ran slowly on to Ratcliff Gorse, near Walton-on-Trent, where he defeated hounds. Thorpe coverts and Statfold blank. Home 5.40 after a very poor day. Strong S.W. wind and cloudy. Rode Golumpus.

On one occasion I found it necessary to write in a more polished manner. I was asked to deputize for the amiable lady who acted as our hunting correspondent in *The Morning Post*. (She also figured in *Horse and Hound*, over the pseudonym ' Tonio ', her real name being Stubbs.)

With Norman's assistance I composed my paragraph in the approved style, making such good use of the material as to earn the caption headline of the column—' Good Day with the Atherstone '. This was the first time any prose of mine appeared in print. More than five years were to pass before I re-emerged as a prose writer, and I was then trying my unpractised hand at ' Literary Notes ' for *The Daily Herald*, of which I had become the literary editor—a Socialist experiment which brought me no credit in the eyes of my fox-hunting friends.

Anyhow my diary never says a word about what happened when I wasn't on horseback. The time at which hounds got home is always meticulously recorded, but I allowed myself no afterthoughts. And there is so little visualized description that one has to make the most of such minor details as ' ran him into Bosworth Park and killed him by the ice-house '—though I find myself unable to remember what the ice-house looked like. ' Only seven got across the brook; Norman fell in but got over, and I went in and out, so the others lost hounds. C. Wiggin bathed! ' produces a clear mental picture, but ' Found close to Corley and ran nicely to ground at the Daimler Works at Coventry' leaves me mystified. It appears that everything except the actual hunting was casually experienced and taken for granted. I had no time to be introspective, and my observations didn't seem worth putting on paper. The people I met talked about nothing but hunting, and although several of the houses we went to must have contained interesting and beautiful objects I don't remember that I looked at anything with more than a glimmer of intelligence or curiosity. No one expected me to. Norman himself was a conversationalist of limited repertoire, and made rather heavy weather for his hosts when we lunched or dined occasionally with influential supporters of the hunt. He went there to talk about their foxes, not to admire their heirlooms. Ex-Masters—of the Hunt—were more in his line than Old Masters. As for me, I was merely a friend and appendage of the M.F.H.'s, with a delusively rich name which was more an embarrassment than an asset. It was all very well, for the time being, to be treated as a young man of ample means and no apparent occupation, and there were moments when my presumed prosperity afforded me a sort of fictitious contentment. But the thought of returning to Kent in the spring was too suggestive of Cinderella coming home from the ball, since it was obvious that I couldn't continue my present glories next season. The idea of hunting with any hounds except Norman's was—as he would have said—' too terrible sad for words ', and I did my best not to think about it.

Meanwhile my four horses were carrying me well. But it wasn't always possible to get four days a week out of them, and I was occasionally to be seen getting my two guineas'-worth from some willing old quad I'd hired from a farmer. After Christmas I began to be somewhat over careful of Cockbird, for fear that he might be incapacitated from competing in the point-to-points, though they weren't till the end of March. I took to riding so wide of hounds that Norman more than once inquired wherever I'd got to when they were running so nicely. It must be added that I preferred to be well away from the crowd. For one thing the majority of them talked too much and paid too little attention to what was happening while hounds were drawing. Also it suited me to cruise about circumspectively on Crusader, who jumped like a deer, but was so badly gone in the wind that he had to be pulled up after galloping a mile or two. There was yet another motive, as the season progressed, for my canny method of following the hunt. I was beginning to feel the need to be alone with my thoughts. For much as I enjoyed my existence at Witherley Lodge, it allowed me little opportunity to meditate or make use of my mind. I hadn't read a book of any kind since I left home. Except for the sporting papers, no printed matter was ever perused at Witherley Lodge. There were times when I felt that my physical fitness was almost a burden, and wondered how long it would take me to regain my mental activity.

Before leaving the subject of my diary I may as well mention that there was a time—more than twenty-five years ago—when I read it over and over again. Returning to the Front from my first leave, I took it with me as an aid to reflection while out of the trenches. In those days its scanty details were very much more evocative than now. Discomfort—and the chance that I might never hear the horn again—endowed the diary with heart-easing capabilities. There was something between those pages which anyhow couldn't be taken away from me; and even a very bad day from Barton-in-the-Beans became an experience to be looked back on with luxuriating regret. Also, while I lay in my sleeping-bag on the floor of some damp and draughty billet, I could make a rough estimate of what life can do in the way of treating one to ups and downs. I may even have allowed myself to compare my conditions with that dizzy ingly good dance at Thorpe Hall, when the whole county assembled for the climax of a period of peace and prosperity. Could one's mud-soaked mind have contemplated the memory of arriving at Thorpe after a long drive in the dark—the subdued but comfortable smell of oil-stoves warming the spacious precincts and passages—the bright and floral ballroom and the admirable band—not to speak of the pervasive aroma of a superexcellent supper? Let us hope that I succeeded in feeling heroic, and reminded myself that I was doing my bit to keep that sort of thing on its legs in the future, even though it contained no place for me!

# XI

By the middle of February my horses' legs were showing signs of the effect of four months' uninterrupted hunting. They would none of them be any the worse for a week's rest, remarked Richardson; and at the same time he probably took it upon himself to remind me that ' the mistress '—as he always called my mother—wouldn't be sorry to see me after I'd been away so long.

My conscience had already hinted that she might be a bit lonely, since both my brothers were abroad—one in British Columbia and the other in the Argentine. I therefore made such arrangements as suited my own inclinations, which resulted in a decision to stay a couple of nights at home and the remainder of the week at my London club. My social engagements in town, though scanty, were by no means nugatory in literary import. For I had been invited to dinner at the Gosses'; and another evening was to be spent with the editor of *Georgian Poetry*, whom I now knew well enough to be able to call him Eddie to his face. I had seen him several times since our first pleasant meeting, and had also received helpful advice about such verses as I had ventured to send him in manuscript, although—as I glumly suspected—they were unworthy of the temperate encouragement that he gave them. Meanwhile I had begun to feel that it was possible to have too much unadulterated fox-hunting, so I looked forward with avidity to hearing from Eddie about the contemporary poets and all that they had been doing lately.

Such being my plans and preparations, it seemed unlikely, when I left Atherstone by the morning train, that anything unforeseen would happen to me before I reached Weirleigh. Something quite unpredictable did, however, occur; and this was brought about by my being obliged to fill in the afternoon somehow, and therefore going to the Hippodrome Revue. I chose the Hippodrome because it would be the most suitable thing to tell Norman I had been to. He would, I knew, derive quiet satisfaction from hearing that I had seen the 'show' which he himself would have selected, instead of dodging away to some high-brow entertainment as soon as he took his eye off me! Anyhow, there I was, ensconced in a stall, much amused by Wilkie Bard's jokes, and mindful of the train I'd got to catch at Charing Cross.

It wasn't until the interval before the last act that the unforeseen took shape. I then became aware of a middle-aged man who was sitting several rows in front of me. Not suspecting that he was anyone I had seen before, I found myself intently observing this clean-shaven cadaverous individual as he turned his head while talking to a woman in a bright red hat who was beside him. Whoever he might be, there was something exceptional—and almost satanic—about his appearance which both interested and repelled me. After a while he seemed to have noticed that I was watching him, for he turned and fixed me with a baleful stare in which I surprisingly detected a hint of recognition.

Where on earth had I seen this extraordinary person before? . . . Surely it couldn't be—and yet it surely must be—yes, it undoubtedly was—neither more nor less than T. W. H. Crosland without his moustache!

While the Revue proceeded to its hilarious finale I was mainly occupied in wondering whether to avoid him or not. He had never given me any cause to dislike him, but the way he had looked at me had been so unpleasant that I assumed it to be the result of my having left unanswered a letter he had sent me about three months before. The letter was written from Monte Carlo, where, he explained, he was ' lying well broken up and without the price of a lunch '. He asked me to send him five pounds, as he didn't know where else to turn. Not having five pounds to throw away, and rather mistrusting the sound of Monte Carlo, I had objected to the idea of my money being spent at a roulette table, though I was unaware that he was—as I afterwards discovered—an inveterate gambler. Nevertheless I couldn't help feeling that, if he really was ill and badly stranded, I ought to have sent him the fiver. He certainly looked ill enough now, as he came slowly up the stalls leaning heavily on a stick. When I had last seen him he had been burly, aggressively confident, and harshly good-humoured. He now looked shrunken, and his expression was lurkingly malevolent. His unexpected apparition was somehow suggestive of a ghastly practical joke. Although I hadn't got any too much time to call for my bag at the club and catch my train, I decided to have a word with him. His manner toward me was stiff but not unfriendly. Feeling a bit uncomfortable about the fiver, I confusedly inquired whether there was any chance of seeing him again. This was merely a figure of speech, but he responded by asking me to lunch with him at Pagani's, which I agreed to do in three days' time, since there seemed no reason for refusing. He had addressed me in a grating undertone which produced an impression that the lunch was a sort of conspiratorial assignation.

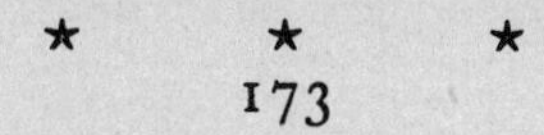

There was so much that I could pour out to my mother about my adventures with the Atherstone that our first evening together passed very happily. Next day, however, the unforeseen asserted itself and reduced everything to desolation. My mother received a telegram telling her that her maid Miriam had died suddenly of heart failure while away on a holiday. Miriam had been with us for many years, and even then I realized her almost saintly willingness to do everybody's work in addition to her own. It was the first time her heart had failed anyone, and she would undoubtedly have rebuked herself for behaving so inconsiderately! Had I heard of her death while up at Atherstone I should have felt sad for a day or two. Riding to the meet, I should have remembered the patient toil she used to spend on getting the mud off my hunting clothes. But I should have defended myself against uncomfortable thoughts of what the news meant to my mother. For her it was the loss not only of a devoted servant but of a noble woman whom she valued with all the depth and loyalty of her nature. Closely involved in this sad situation, I came out of it rather badly. I felt wretchedly helpless and unable to offer any active consolation. I could only bemoan to myself that people had no right to die suddenly and cause all this misery just when my mother and

I were getting on so well. I could do no more than sympathize with her sorrow; and what use was sympathy? It was the kind of experience which one remembers afterwards with vain self-reproaches for one's crudity and callousness. Later on in life one accepts and admits the fact that youthful conduct can be unfeeling in a way that demands our tolerance. Young people don't take things to heart unless their own interests and enterprises are affected by the event. Delicacy isn't there until it has been acquired. One can at any rate be candid about it now. On that forlorn and sunless February afternoon my prevailing desire was to be anywhere but at Weirleigh. At the best of times it would have seemed a little depressing compared with the liveliness of my existence in Warwickshire; but now, while I wandered moodily about the garden, I was conscious of having somehow outgrown the whole place during my absence. One's home was all very well, but one couldn't remain tied to it for ever. My genuine regret that dear old Miriam had departed to a better world didn't dispel my awareness that the prospect of returning home in the spring for an indefinite period was definitely dreary. Sitting by the fire in the Studio, I felt that my collection of books had become stale and unprofitable. The future appeared aimless and inadequate, and I was beginning to be uneasy about it.

Travelling up to town next day by the late afternoon train, with a compartment to myself and my feet on the opposite seat, I felt a bit of a brute to be leaving my mother alone with her sadness, but unreflectively relieved to be putting funereal thoughts behind me. As usual she had made the best of her calamity by saying, at my departure, how nice it was to think that I should be dining at the Gosses' that evening. 'I shall read some of my beloved Meredith,' she added. For the philosophy in his writings was always her sign-post to a courageous acceptance of adversity. It now occurred to me that I hadn't told her about my curious encounter with Crosland, so it wouldn't be possible for her to be with me in spirit at lunch-time next day; which was just as well, I decided, considering the sort of man he was and how unprepossessing he had looked without his moustache! Crosland, however, belonged to unborn to-morrow and could be dismissed from my mind for the time being. What concerned me at the moment was that I must on no account be a minute late for dinner with Mr. Gosse, who had explained in his courteous note of invitation that I should 'find him forsaken by his ladies who were absent from London for a few days'. I was jolly lucky to have been asked there at all, I thought, as I eyed through the carriage window the brown familiar scene of hop-gardens and orchards, with here and there a farm-house showing its friendly light across the watery winter dusk.

I had seen Mr. Gosse but once since our meeting at the House of Lords last March. The occasion had been an evening party at Hanover Terrace, at which I had arrived red-faced from a long day's cricket. I had thoroughly enjoyed the party, and had been made much of by a charming Indian poetess named Sarojini Naidu, but there had been no opportunity for Mr. Gosse to devote more than a few welcoming words to me. To-night would therefore be a considerable augmenting of my acquaintance with him, who had mingled with so many of the majestic immortals—had talked with Tennyson, breakfasted with Browning, and supped with Swinburne—figures whom I found it difficult to think of as existing anywhere except on Parnassus, however much one had studied their earthly biographies. Yes, I cogitated, pulling the window up as the train plunged into Sevenoaks tunnel with a shriek, I was on my way to have dinner with someone who would probably have known Keats and Shelley—or even Shakespeare —if he'd happened to have been born in time for it! And for all I knew I might meet a future immortal there this very evening, since there must be incipient poetic geniuses about the world somewhere if one had the luck to discover them, and Mr. Gosse had always made it his business to do so.

★ ★ ★

It needs no saying that I was far removed from such airy flights of fancy when I sat down to dinner a couple of hours later. The lolling and loose-minded person in the railway carriage was now dumb with decorum and petrified with politeness. There were only three of us at the table. Opposite me was Mr. Filson Young, whom I knew of as the author of a novel called *The Sands of Pleasure*. He looked to be about ten years older than myself, and was self-possessed and mature in manner. Behind him was the vivid profile portrait of Mr. Gosse which Sargent had painted before I was born.

The meal began with a minor mistake on my part which serves well to illustrate my confused mental condition. Mr. Gosse, with emphatic archness, intimated that he was expecting me to give my fullest appreciation to his hermitage. Dimly wondering why he was referring to his house in Regent's Park as a hermitage and why he pronounced the word with a sort of French accent, I replied—with stupefied jocosity—that it seemed to be a nice big one! 'Not unbecomingly large, I hope,' he somewhat tartly replied, looking inquiringly at the bottle in front of him from which he was about to fill our glasses. I thus became aware of my misinterpretation, for the name on the label was, of course, Hermitage. I awkwardly explained my indistinct assumption that he had been describing himself as a hermit because Mrs. Gosse was away. But in spite of his graceful and amused acceptance of my blunder I felt that Filson Young must regard me as next door to an imbecile. And in my anxiety to gain favour with Mr. Gosse I probably took a most unconnoisseurish gulp of the revered vintage. Anyhow, my sense of being, to some extent, there on probation made this incident seem worse than it was, and thenceforward my contributions to the conversation were acquiescent and unventuresome. This was facilitated for me by the fact that the other two could obviously have got on just as well—or even better—if I hadn't been there at all. Meanwhile Mr. Gosse turned from one to the other of us in his attempts to include both in his talk, but coalescence between Filson Young and myself never seemed to be effected. There were evidently a number of things which he desired to discuss with his host, and I was merely an impediment to the proceedings. Of the two, Filson Young was much the more deliberate in his utterances. His voice was tinged with orotundity, and most of his remarks appeared to have been preconsidered. I felt that he was quite an agreeable man, but too editorial in tone.

At that time he was prominent in London journalism through a very successful half-column of paragraphs in one of the evening papers. I had often read—and immediately forgotten—under the heading *The Things that Matter*, what Filson Young considered them to be. He did it from day to day, with urbane ability, and people going home in the train derived satisfaction from the performance. He was now, as it were, trying a few of them over on Mr. Gosse, who would—it struck me—have preferred topics to move a shade faster, for as the evening wore on he showed an increasing tendency to discuss the things that didn't matter quite so much as long as they were amusing.

I remember that soon after we went upstairs to the drawing-room Filson Young pinned him down to an exchange of ideas on the problem of punctuation. I listened with modest alertness while they agreed that it was a matter to which many writers devoted far too little attention. This took me by surprise, since I had never thought about it at all, and had no notion that it made any difference in the art of writing. Filson Young had put it to Mr. Gosse—toward whom he was extremely deferential—that the use of punctuation was essentially personal; but I regarded myself as having no aptitude for prose, and assumed that poetry didn't enter into the question. Anyhow, I would much rather have heard Mr. Gosse's personal remembrances of the famous punctuators themselves as he had known them in the past, or have been given a glimpse of some eminent ones who were still alive.

At this point, however, he took flight from the subject by darting to a book-case, whence he returned holding up a volume with a circular gilt device on its dark blue binding. Here, he announced, was a little masterpiece which we writers could ponder with perennial attention—parody irradiated by critical divination of the finest quality. Of course, he continued, we were both of us fully familiar with *A Christmas Garland.* His only complaint was that he could never be sure which of the pieces in it he relished most.

'Perhaps my own Christmas dinner with Ibsen and Browning,' he intimated, gazing rather roguishly in our direction.

Filson Young, on being asked his favourite, plumped for *The Mote in the Middle Distance,* which prompted Mr. Gosse to relate how Henry James—after a Christmas dinner two months ago—had roamed round that very room discussing 'with extraordinary vivacity and appreciation—not only the superlative intelligence of the book as a whole, but *The Mote in the Middle Distance* itself, which he had read in a self-scrutinizing bewilderment of wonder and admiration'.

I may add that, had my own preference among the parodies been asked for, I should have been obliged to agree with Mr. Gosse that it was impossible to say—a statement which would have contained a simulacrum of truth, because, except for Meredith, Kipling and Wells, I knew little or nothing about the writers parodied, and was as yet unacquainted with the contents of *A Christmas Garland*, though I have read it many times since, with amplified enjoyment.

But I was now being shown something of the real Edmund Gosse. Alight with an almost youthful enthusiasm, he seemed to enrich the room with a glow reflected from ideal regions of classic achievement, and I felt highly privileged when he rolled forth a few passages from the 'Garland' in tones of racy expressiveness and resonant authority.

'Dear delicious Max,' he exclaimed as he closed the book, 'Would that he had been with us this evening!' He then bent forward to stir the fire with a slightly impatient movement; after which—greatly to my regret—he glanced upward at the massive marble clock on the mantelpiece. The hour being almost ten-thirty, there was nothing discourteous in this reminder that we were due to depart. We had most indulgently redeemed his domestic desolation, he assured us, but it must be remembered that an aged gentleman ought not to sit up too late. As we walked away outside the lamplit arcade of Hanover Terrace, my fellow guest remarked that Gosse at sixty-five was the liveliest old gentleman he knew. He himself had seemed rather the reverse. But it has since occurred to me that his somewhat portentous demeanour may have been caused by his being quite as much on his best behaviour as I was.

## XII

When keeping my appointment with Crosland I could at any rate be sure that it would provide a contrasted experience to the previous night's dinner. I even felt some doubt whether he would be there at all, so fortuitous and peculiar had our Hippodrome encounter been, and so seemingly incongruous it was for him to have invited me to lunch. Anyhow, there he was, awaiting me in Pagani's Restaurant, and out wardly less morose in mood, for he greeted me with something which resembled geniality. At the moment he hadn't much to say, since he was evidently treating the meal itself as a serious matter. We sat down to a large round table in an unfrequented corner. The table was big enough for half a dozen people, which felt rather queer at first—with Crosland such a long way off and saying so little. Later on, however, it seemed appropriate that we should have so much elbow-room, and gave the proceedings an almost lordly atmosphere. We were plentifully supplied with hors d'œuvres, but he made short work of them and replenished his plate. While assiduously following his example I wondered what else he had ordered.

It hadn't occurred to me when I arrived there that the meal I was in for would be anything exceptional. But I am now confident in asserting that it was just about the largest lunch I have ever eaten in my life. In fact it can only be described as a gorge.

Pagani portions were always bountiful. In later years I often dined there when on my way to Queen's Hall, and I learnt by experience that one portion sufficed for two ordinary concert-goers. On this occasion Crosland must have paid for double portions, judging by the astonishing quantity of Jugged Hare which was put before us. There was also a large flask of Chianti, which went well with it, and by the time I was half-way through my second glass I felt quite chummy with Crosland, whose countenance now looked gauntly convivial, though he remained unresponsive to my attempts to make him talk. When I asked whether he was going to start another literary magazine he merely replied, 'Have some more'—pointing to the residue of the Jugged Hare with a fully-charged fork and adding, in an unsmiling afterthought, 'The people here give you all you want for your money'. This remark was substantiated by the dimensions of our next course, which gave an impression that the waiter had overlooked the fact that only two persons were at the table instead of half a dozen. The mound of Pêche Melba which he carried was so stupendous that it really seemed as if there must be some mistake. But Crosland's only comment was to ask for a larger spoon. Having shovelled in a few mouthfuls he announced—more to himself than to me—' This is lovely '. Anyone watching us for the next ten or fifteen minutes might well have concluded that we were doing it for a bet. My recollection is that we finished about all square. He got it down quickest, but I maintained a steady pace which enabled me to stay the course to the last liquefying spoonful. He had made no allusion to the excessive amount we were consuming.

' What do you do after a meal like this? ' I inquired, leaning back in my chair and unobtrusively releasing a few waistcoat buttons.

' I eat nothing at all for twenty-four hours, ' he replied, signalling to the waiter and ordering special coffee and a couple of Corona cigars.

Observed in retrospect, that luncheon looms out almost like an invented improbability. I must have felt something of the sort at the time, for he was so altered from my previous impressions of him that I could scarcely believe that he was the bluntly outspoken editor with a thick moustache who had struck me as formidable but roughly genial. The north-country accent was there, but otherwise the man was perplexingly different. Temporarily affable—while finishing the Chianti, which I had made over to him after my second glass—this clean-shaven Crosland, with lank hair thinning away from his forehead, pouched and heavy-lidded eyes, and sullenly uncompromising mouth—could one regard him as other than vaguely sinister and disreputable? Was the wicked look in that saturnine face to be accounted for by broken health and the failure of his gambling system at Monte Carlo—for he had tersely explained that his system had let him down, after dismissing my regrets for the unanswered letter with a wave of his cigar? Supposing—I may have thought—we were to be joined by someone open-minded and sagacious—could I convince such an observer that my companion wasn't a bit of a blackguard? I might, of course, make the best of it by explaining that he was—or had been—my publisher. But the obvious inquiry 'Has he ever paid you anything?' could only have been answered to Crosland's disadvantage.

Anyhow, there we were, and in the light of subsequent knowledge of his habits I take leave to suggest that we were the most incongruous couple of literary men to be seen together that day in London.

I was feeling somewhat stupefied by the amount of food I'd eaten, but my publisher appeared impervious to the effects of the meal, and I now tried to get him going on a few opinions about contemporary authors, hoping for something in the style of his domineering and derisive articles. This he declined to give. But being much mellowed in general behaviour, he became expansively eloquent about human experience as a whole. He began by remarking that although he envied me my ignorance of the infamies of my fellow men, he found nothing worth wishing for in my comfortable circumstances. Life, he explained with increasing vehemence, ought to be a Promethean struggle with adversity and injustice. Those who had never been down into the pit and suffered the stings and arrows of outrageous fortune couldn't claim to have lived at all.

Politely assuming that his opinions were largely impersonal and not intended to apply literally to myself, I listened with sympathetic gravity while he pictured his own career, which offered, apparently, the spectacle of a man contending against unfavourable odds and grimly rejoicing in his peck of troubles. I knew nothing of his past history as a private individual, though I have since been told that he was a man of intemperate habits, improvidently generous in times of prosperity, and that he endured severe hardships and deprivations in his early days as an underpaid journalist. But I was aware that he had frequently indulged in virulent litigation, and I concluded that this counted as a Promethean exercise in spiritual purgation, and that making a host of enemies by writing blistering reviews of books came into the same category of the human drama.

Later on in his monologue he made me feel slightly embarrassed by moralizing about the contrast between what he was now and what he had been in his days of angel innocence. No doubt he spoke quite genuinely, but his exalted sentiments concerning the holiness of motherhood and the redeeming influence of the domestic virtues didn't harmonize with his personal appearance, a large-sized liqueur brandy, and the stub end of a fat cigar. Much more in character was his concluding assertion that his most frequent prayer had been 'Good Lord deliver me from the dangers of respectability'. I found no difficulty in believing that his prayer had been answered; but there was also something about him which made it possible to imagine him preaching fervently from a nonconformist pulpit. Meanwhile he positively gloried in the prospect of battling against ill-health and insolvency.

'Giving hard knocks and getting them in

return—that's my game!' he remarked. 'I wasn't born to be charitable to anyone except the downtrodden and the destitute.'

Whereupon he finished his brandy and proceeded to pay the bill with a nice new five-pound note. Considering that I was neither downtrodden nor destitute, it seemed inconsistent for him to have been standing me such an expensive lunch. But Crosland's character must have been mainly composed of contradictions. How many of the ingredients were honourable ones it is needless to inquire. We parted amicably on the pavement outside Pagani's, and he moved stoopingly away, supporting himself on a stick. I never saw him again or felt any further inclination to communicate with him.

* * *

Although my club in St. James's Street had solid merits, liveliness was not among them. By comparison the Bath Club, to which I sometimes went with Norman, was a vortex of youthful festivity. On entering my club I instinctively assumed a gravity of deportment suitable to my surroundings. In fact it made me feel fully five years older than my age, which at that time seemed a great deal. On the present occasion, however, I was in the mood to be quiet, and found nothing depressing in the place being almost deserted by nine o'clock in the evening.

There was a library at the top of the house, and I had discovered that the members used it very little, so I knew that if I went up there after dinner there was every chance that I should be undisturbed. On the next two nights I took full advantage of this. The room was small but pleasant to sit in, the library a moderately good one, a bright fire was burning, and during the past five months I'd had few opportunities of being cosily alone with my naturally meditative mind. Thus the first evening slipped luxuriously away. The after-effects of the Pagani luncheon weren't conducive to mental animation, but I spent several hours between the library ladder and a large leather arm-chair, dipping into various friendly volumes and disturbing the dust of the top shelves, oblivious to everything except my enjoyment in being let loose among a decent collection of books. Up there long after midnight, with a green-shaded lamp beside me and the diminishing drone of the traffic far below, I felt that I could do with a lot more of this sort of thing, and my sense of detachment from my sporting acquaintances was almost disquietingly delightful.

On the following evening, after spending a dull and solitary Sunday, I went up to the library with an emptily lethargic mind and sat for some time without even bothering to get a book. My subsequent experience was therefore as unexpected as it was mentally eruptive. I can summarize it by saying that it was as though all my accumulated physical energy had gone to my head and were instigating a rebellion against the months of intellectual and emotional suppression which I had undergone at Atherstone. It seemed that I was bursting with something to express, but had no idea how to do it. I felt that I ought to set to work on a tremendous poem full of prophetic sublimity, spiritual aspiration, and human tragedy, and that I needed to begin my life all over again and give up everything except being noble and uplifting. I also wanted to be heroic; for like most undisillusioned people I had often imagined that I might some day get a chance to be a hero, though I didn't realize that heroism and histrionics aren't the same thing. Those two or three hours, in fact, contained an embodiment of my confused and incoherent feelings about 'the unknown want, the destiny of me'. I probably put it to myself, in a loose way, that my immortal soul was reminding me of its immaterial responsibilities and demanding freedom of action. For I was still a long way from having learnt that it is wiser to leave 'the soul' to the philosophers than to claim it as a personal possession. And I had yet to ask (in the words of a fine poet who was also Attorney-General to Queen Elizabeth)

*For why should we the busy Soul believe,*
*When boldly she concludes of that and this;*
*When of her self she can no Judgment give,*
*Nor how, nor whence, nor where, nor what she is?*

From a practical point of view, of course, what I needed was a spell of solitude and invigorative reading. I was suffering from an overdose of reynardism, which wasn't permanently compatible with my temperament, beneficial though it had been to my character and constitution.

★ ★ ★

While dining with Eddie Marsh next day I could think of very little worth saying about what I had done since I last saw him. I wasn't there to talk about hunting, even if he had cared to hear such details. I made the most of my evening with Mr. Gosse, but was discreetly silent about that notoriously unpresentable person Crosland. Eddie, however, was refreshingly communicative about the Georgian poets and the literary world in general, and—after I had mentioned the *Christmas Garland*—gave me an admirable imitation of Henry James searching for the exact word he wanted in one of his parenthetical and pauseful discourses. It was delightful to feel that he liked me personally, though I was conscious of having failed to justify the interest in my work which he had shown when I first met him. Equally delightful was the impression he gave of being so much less than fourteen years my senior and of having retained his full capacity for youthful enjoyment.

After an excellent dinner at the Moulin d'Or we went to his flat in Gray's Inn. I had been there before, but it had never seemed such an attractive place as it did now, when I was in the mood to contrast it with my less civilized surroundings in Warwickshire. The rooms contained everything that was lacking at Witherley Lodge, and while inspecting the modern pictures he had collected —some of them a bit beyond me until their merits were explained—I felt that my recent existence had been altogether too Philistine and one-sided. Evidence of exquisite taste and selective enterprise was around me, while Eddie himself, with his alert enthusiasm, made all the arts alive with the freshness of discovery. It was the Gosse atmosphere in a different guise, stimulating and rich with refinements, and once again I became conscious that there were far too many things in the literary and artistic world which I ought to have heard of and hadn't.

This led me to refer somewhat dolefully to the state of mental stagnation from which I had been suffering. Leaning back in an arm-chair and lighting my pipe, I remarked in my most humourless manner that I had absolutely nothing to look forward to after the hunting season except playing cricket and writing unsatisfactory sonnets. This was intended to be merely a statement of a mournful but unalterable eventuality. The unforeseen, however, had a surprise in store for me in Eddie's unhesitating reply.

'But why don't you come and live in London?' he exclaimed. 'You can't expect all the interesting things to come down and stay with you in Kent!'

It did just cross my mind that I ought to explain how my financial position compelled me to stay at home and economize; but his solution had caused such an instant sense of future liberation that I only demurred weakly by saying that I hadn't much idea of how to find a place in London where I could live. When he suggested Gray's Inn I knew that the matter was as good as settled, and left my scruples to take care of themselves. In less than five minutes an inspiriting prospect had been opened out for me, and I had found an escape from my mental perplexities in the club library.

Eddie was now in his element, and overflowing with helpfulness. He undertook to make the necessary inquiries and would telephone to me about it in the morning. Thus I ended the evening optimistic and elated, and returned to my club convinced that I had taken a long stride in the right direction. When Eddie rang me up after breakfast to say that there was a vacant set of rooms on the top floor in the same block of buildings as his own, I felt that it would take a lot to prevent them meeting with my approval. We lunched at a restaurant in Whitehall and then hurried off to inspect them.

It must be admitted that, at first sight, the rooms met my hopefulness much less than halfway. One had to allow for their being empty and depressingly dilapidated, but even so they looked drearier than anything I had foreseen. Eddie, however, assured me that when redecorated and furnished they would be unrecognizably improved. Redecoration was a matter which hadn't entered into my calculations; but the need for it was so indisputable that I gratefully accepted his offer to get it all done for me without delay. How should I have managed without him, I wondered, not having as yet realized his unlimited capability for befriending the poets.

While my train was carrying me back to the

Midlands I mused complacently on the easy way in which everything had been arranged. There was nothing else to do now except sign an agreement with the Gray's Inn authorities for their stipulated three years' lease and wait for the estimate from the decorator who was going to work such wonders with the desperately dingy interior of my future abode. I hadn't inquired of Eddie how much he thought it would cost, but I knew that the rent of the rooms came to a hundred a year including rates and taxes. My hopeful assumption was that redecoration wouldn't be more than another hundred, at the worst. Mindful of the fact that I was already keeping four horses, Richardson, and a stable helper, on an income of less than six hundred a year, and that I also had a lot of unpaid bills, I experienced a few moments of mental discomfort about the expense of furnishing the rooms. But it was too late to begin worrying about that, so I dismissed the matter with an inward exclamation—' Blast the money! What I want is to get out of my groove '.

* * *

On returning to Witherley I found no difficulty in resuming my existence there as though I had done nothing unexpected during my absence.

There was no need for me to describe those doings to anyone. I merely came back to find Norman carving a joint of beef and Wiggin relating what had been happening while I was away with his usual sprightliness. My diary laconically records that I had missed two of the best hunts of the season; and the day after my return I was out with the hounds at No Man's Heath, having 'a nice thirty minutes from Newton Gorse, by Appleby', followed by 'twenty minutes, fast, from Barnacles to Orton and back to Grendon Hall and killed him'. In fact I seem to have made up for lost time, for I was out hunting six days in the next eight. Among them was the memorable one on which Norman took his hounds by special train to an invitation day in the Pytchley country. A small but resolute contingent of Atherstonians accompanied him, and there was a fine concourse of fashionable sporting folk at the meet. Never had I beheld such a well-dressed crowd, but much the most distinctive figure among them was a monumental old gentleman mounted on a sturdy cob and wearing patent-leather boots which came above his knees. I gazed at him with awed curiosity, for it was 'the Squire of Blankney', Henry Chaplin, immediately recognizable from the triple-chinned parliamentary caricatures of him in *Punch*.

It is nice to remember the benignant modesty with which he introduced himself to Norman. 'The Squire' was well over seventy and too heavy to ride to hounds any more, and there was something touching in the way this renowned sportsman—who had run through his fortune in the grand style—greeted one of the leaders of the younger generation. Norman responded, with shy respectfulness, by saying that he was 'terrible pleased' to meet him, and the great Mr. Chaplin then inspected the Atherstone bitch pack with a monocled and urbanely appraiseful eye.

The day's hunting was good, though not remarkable, as none of the foxes ran straight. The country was the best I had ever ridden across, and Cockbird sailed over an uncomputable series of well-trimmed fences in a sea of grass. My most vivid mental picture in the day is of Charles Wiggin, after the first fox had been found, galloping past me with an agonized countenance, having bumped his knee violently against a gate-post in his death-or-glory determination to 'show the white collars the way'. Anyhow, we re-boxed the hounds and horses at Lamport, feeling well satisfied with our performance, and 'Home 9.30!' was duly recorded in my diary. Tired, no doubt, we were; but off again next morning for a fourteen-mile hack to the meet and a long day in the Wednesday plough country. Wonderful indeed seems that heedless energy of twenty-eight years ago! . . .

Our point-to-point races, which were about a fortnight later, provided a suitable climax to the season. It was an eventful day. Norman won the Light-Weight race from a field of sixteen runners, but only did so through the two horses who finished in front of him being disqualified for going the wrong side of a flag—whereby, it must be added, they gained about fifty lengths from him. I figured unobtrusively on gallant old ' Rubicon ', who came in a bad fourth, but—as Richardson proudly remarked—' as full of running as he was when he started '. This staying power of his we always sententiously attributed to the fact that he was a descendant of the famous ' Blair Athol '. Anyhow, he must have been the oldest horse in the race, for he was nearly twenty.

The Heavy-Weight race ought to have been won by H. A. Brown—one of the greatest amateur riders of his time. But he was on a rather inferior jumper, and fell two fences from the end when leading by a distance, leaving Norman and myself to contest a very close finish, during which we weren't moving nearly so fast as some of the spectators imagined, and which resulted in Cockbird winning by not much more than the length of his neck.

## XIII

Latch-key in hand, I went briskly up the twisty stone stairway to the fourth floor of 1 Raymond Buildings. It was my first night there, so I stood for a moment looking at my name, painted in neat letters above the outer door, the solidity of which I observed with proprietary satisfaction. Having entered and closed the door with luxuriating deliberation, I surveyed the interior as though for the first time. There was my immaculate white bedroom; the brightly-renovated bathroom; and the main room with its windows overlooking the terraced lawns and tall plane trees of Gray's Inn gardens. Very pleasant it all seemed, in the fading light of a fine evening in the first week of May. Quiet too, and almost collegiate, except for the clank and jangle of an electric tram rumbling along Theobald's Road. (My rooms were at the noisiest end of the Buildings, which was perhaps why I had been able to obtain them so easily; but one wouldn't hear the traffic so much when the windows were shut.) Anyhow my good-sized peacock-blue room was waiting for me to add a chapter to its previous history, whereof I knew nothing except the name of the former occupant—a detail which I am now unable to remember! Peacock-blue had been selected because it was my favourite colour: a touch of gold would have lightened the general effect, but it looked delightful as it was; and so did the small room adjoining it, for which I had chosen French grey, though there was nothing in it at present, unless one counted the window-seat as furniture. So far the flat contained very little, and the uncarpeted floors made it sound somewhat unlived-in. Carpets were things which hadn't occurred to me, and my two small rugs didn't seem to make much difference. Unwilling to find fault with anything, but with an eye for possible improvements, I wondered whether the room really needed more than the two chairs and the sofa which were doing their best not to look solitary. The sofa at any rate was very comfortable, with one end that could be let down when you wanted your head lower. It was like reposing on a cloud, my mother had remarked when I brought her to inspect my abode a few days before. The carved oak chest looked just right against the wall between the windows, I decided, listening to the rosewood clock striking nine. The clock had been more expensive than I'd intended, but it had an almost inaudible tick and a discreetly melodious chime. Behind it, above the mantelpiece, hung my only picture, a good German colour reproduction of Titian's grave young man with a glove. He and I had the place to ourselves, and his calm scrutiny gave me a vague sense of loneliness, which I overcame by thinking that the slight smell of paint and floor-polish made the room feel clean and friendly. There was also a perceptible odour of recent plumbing from the bathroom, but it didn't seem to me at all unpleasant. Nothing could alter the fact that this was my flat and nobody else's!

Meanwhile there was all that white lilac which my mother had insisted on my bringing up from Weirleigh; this led to the discovery that I had nothing to put it in except the bedroom water-jug. But it was a blue and white willow-pattern one and did very well, and what was left over went into the basin.

It only needs my piano here to make it perfect, I said to myself; but the idea of hiring one was extinguished by the thought of my ever-impending overdraft. Piano-playing, however, wasn't what I'd come to London for. I was going to counteract cricket and hunting by leading an enterprising existence which would give me something real to write about. To show that I was making a fresh start I had brought no books with me, except for the small Oxford dictionary which was on my table between a sheet of clean blotting-paper and a folio edition of Gray's poems with engraved designs which I'd bought that afternoon in Bond Street without consciously connecting it with Gray's Inn.

The evening had now turned a bit chilly: one could almost do with a fire, I thought, as I shut the windows, drew the brown-gold curtains (the only thing I'd borrowed from Weirleigh), and switched on the ceiling light. A couple of candles would have suited me better; I must remember to buy some to-morrow, and also a sensible reading-lamp. One felt rather too public in this white glare from above. I then made myself some tea. Everything in the kitchen had been beautifully arranged by Mrs. Fretter, whose daily services had been secured for me by Eddie's housekeeper and paragon of perfections, Mrs. Elgy. Having baptized the tea-pot, there seemed nothing left for me to do except read Gray's Elegy, which I already knew backwards. So I preferred to puff my pipe on the sofa, calmly considering such plans as I had for the immediate future. To begin with, every morning I intended to put in two or three hours at my table, making up for the time I had lost by doing so little writing during the past year. Both Mr. Gosse and Eddie had urged me to take a more lively interest in the technique of verse, and I meant to follow their advice, not bothering about lack of inspiration. Thus no morning would be wasted, and before long, I hoped, I should become poetically productive and there would be something worth submitting to Eddie. That he lived almost within shouting distance of me at the other end of the Buildings was an incentive. How splendid it would be if I were able to stroll up to his rooms with a second *Daffodil Murderer* in my pocket, only this time it must be something strikingly modern and original, both in style and subject! This led to a roseate vision of my potential poem appearing in the second 'Georgian' anthology which was in process of formation for publication next year. The use I was going to make of my afternoons and evenings was less easy to meditate upon. One had to put one's faith in unforeseen events, such as getting to know plenty of people who might involve me in their interesting activities. Apart from that it would be quite an occupation for me merely to explore London, and there were always the picture galleries and museums to fall back on when I felt like it. There was also watching a bit of cricket at Lord's or the Oval, an idea which I dismissed as inappropriate though not unpalatable. The main trouble was that I hadn't enough money to be continually going to concerts and theatres, and I should have to try and go somewhere after dinner, since it would be rather depressing to come straight home with nothing to do except read a book. It was too much to hope that I should find myself sitting up till the small hours writing a masterpiece. Meanwhile London was around me—a purposeful drone of traffic under the summer sky. My future, I felt, was written in its stars. I was young, and it didn't seem anything like seven years since I had come down from Cambridge, possibly because I had done so little since then. Here I was, anyhow, falling asleep on the sofa unless I heaved myself up and went to bed.

★ ★ ★

In those first days of my London summer I used to awake with a sense of freedom and exhilaration. It was the right time of year for feeling like that, and my fresh start in new surroundings seemed much the same as the outset of a holiday. I did not ask myself what I had done to deserve a holiday or what I was having a holiday from! All I knew was that the sunshine looked auspicious and the trees jubilantly green. It was difficult to imagine a December fog outside the windows or anything unlucky happening inside them.

I liked Mrs. Fretter, who was young and pleasant-faced and did things in a shy unobtrusive way; I liked the aroma of frying bacon and well-made coffee; I liked the company of my own mind and the certainty that I couldn't be interfered with. So altogether there was every reason for me to be singing while I was having a cold bath.

After a leisurely breakfast there was my moderately industrious morning ahead of me, though studying poetry with the purpose of finding out how it ought to be done in cold blood led to a certain amount of wool-gathering, gazing out of the window, and strolling around the room with an eye on the clock.

Subsequently—at about twelve-thirty—I should go forth from Raymond Buildings in an almost new black jacket, with my blurless top-hat slightly tilted at the appropriately jaunty angle, neatly-rolled umbrella hooked over the left arm, and a pair of clean wash-leather gloves in the right hand. Thus attired, to take a 19 or 38 bus as far as Piccadilly Circus and then saunter along to St. James's Street was, apparently, the correct way for me to make my appearance in the West End of London. (In rainy weather I should revert to my blue suit and bowler.) At present, however, I had no need of an engagement-book, and my emergences led to nothing more than having lunch with myself at my club. This I had once heard jocularly misnamed 'The United Nonentities', and although I had belonged to it for nearly seven years I had seldom spoken to anyone except the hall-porter and the head-waiter. I was now on nodding terms with one or two elderly habitués, whom I suspected of being considerable bores if one gave them a chance. It seemed that when hanging up my top-hat at the club I was a sort of hybrid product of my ' double-life ' during the past few years. One half of me was hunting-field and the other was gentleman writer. Perusing the papers after lunch I should be equally engrossed by yesterday's cricket and racing in *The Sportsman* and in whatever ' poetry and belles lettres ' I could discover in the current periodicals. Now and again I vaguely speculated as to what the other occupants of the smoking-room did with themselves during the afternoon. None of them looked as if they had anything urgent to go out for. I myself should be walking about in search of a few oddments to improve my rooms, this still being just enough to make me feel that I'd got something to do.

My evenings remained a bit of a problem. But I was going to hear *The Magic Flute* the day after to-morrow, and Eddie Marsh had asked me to dine with him one day next week and go to a concert performance of Handel's *Acis and Galatea*, which sounded unexciting but would no doubt be good for me. It was no use expecting a lot of things to happen all of a sudden, and I found it quite good fun wandering about by myself.

* * *

By the time I had been in London five weeks I was realizing that my plans weren't working out so fruitfully as I'd expected. For one thing I had made very poor use of my mornings. Unable to write a line of poetry, I found that unmethodical investigations of verse technique only resulted in a persistent feeling that I should do better to be out of doors instead of burying my nose in a book. I was feeling almost inconveniently healthy, and my imagination appeared to have dried up altogether. Nor were my afternoons notably satisfying in their outcome. A couple of conscientious visits to the National Gallery had for the time being exhausted my interest in Old Masters. Looking at one object after another at the British and South Kensington Museums had shown that I had no sufficiently definite purpose for such sight-seeing: everything that I inspected was cancelled out by what I looked at next, and I came away in a state of unremembering fatigue. ' Thou shalt not wilt ' seemed to be the most suitable words to inscribe above the entrance to a Museum.

I was no great judge of architecture, but my pilgrimage to St. Paul's had stimulated me into surmounting several hundred steps to the topmost parapet of the Dome, whence I had obtained a clear view of the City churches and the dark green of the distant Kentish hills. And after descending I had paid my respects to Uncle Hamo's bronze figure of Bishop Creighton, which gave me its patriarchal blessing in one of the side aisles. But one couldn't spend more than a limited number of one's afternoons in cathedrals, and I don't remember that I betook myself to Westminster Abbey.

I had ceased to awake in the morning with that pleasant feeling of indefinite expectancy; I was beginning to lose heart about wearing my top-hat on fine days; and my daily routine had indeed become more and more a matter of going out and trying not to feel at a loose end. Several times I had been reduced to boarding an omnibus just to see what sort of places it went to. One of them took me to Hornsey Rise, whence I returned unrewarded. On another I was more fortunately conveyed to Kew Gardens, where I had quite a refreshing ramble, although I had previously thought of it as a place only to be enjoyed by gardeners.

In my explorations of the Gray's Inn locality I was still more than likely to lose my way when less than half-a-mile from home. One dull afternoon toward the end of May, having got as far as what I conjectured to be Camden Town, I accidentally discovered Regent's Park, which I hadn't suspected of being anywhere near there. After I'd walked across to the ornamental water I became aware that I was quite close to Hanover Terrace, so I decided that I might as well call on the Gosses, though I still regarded Mr. Gosse as too momentous a man to be approached without ceremonious preliminaries. There could be no harm, however, in leaving my card. I happened to have one on me in case I lost my memory or got run over by a cab. Mr. Gosse was almost certain to be at the House of Lords Library, and if Mrs. Gosse were at home she would be glad to get some news of my mother. The result of my call was a disappointment. Someone whom I assumed to be the cook, after peering at me through one of the dining-room windows, emerged to inform me that 'Mr. and Mrs. Gosse had gone off to Portugal and would be absent from home for another four weeks'. I'm not making much headway at Hanover Terrace, I thought, remembering how my mother and I had gone there to tea about two months before. For a while we had been alone with Mrs. Gosse, and then Mr. George Moore had been unexpectedly announced. I had read nothing by him, but I knew that my mother detested his novels and had taken a strong dislike to him when she had met him in her youth. On this occasion Mr. Moore monopolized the conversation, indulging in a long jeremiad against the uncivilized habits of dogs on door-steps. He had lately returned from the Holy Land, and gave us a memorable description of the blisters he got on his behind while riding from Joppa to Jerusalem on a mule. He had struck me as being a peculiarly unpleasant old gentleman who also happened to be doing his best to be at his worst. Anyhow poor Mrs. Gosse's tea-party had been no success at all, and my mother had been speechless with indignation when Mr. Moore informed us that Dickens didn't know how to write.

And now, I thought, as I glumly threaded my way among the perambulators and nurse-maids by the ornamental water, the Gosses had gone to Portugal and there was no chance of my seeing them before the end of June.

★ ★ ★

What else had I done with myself during those first few weeks in London? . . . Nothing that I can now remember except the Sale of the Atherstone Hunt horses. But the Sale had been merely a belated good-bye to the best and jolliest hunting season I'd ever experienced. On that grilling hot day in Derby Week Tattersall's Yard had been crowded with friendly Atherstone faces, and quite a lot of people had invited me to look them up while they were in London. In one case there had even been a charmingly artless assumption that I should be discoverable in the Royal Enclosure at Ascot. I had spent the greater part of the morning dutifully and confidentially cracking-up Norman's horses to a succession of inquirers, all of whom regarded me as ' in the know ' and attempted to pump me, not so much about their merits as their defects.

It had been one of those strenuously subsidiary days which were typical of my association with Norman Loder. I didn't do much, but I was trying my best to be helpful, dawdling about in the stables and the sale yard while the monotone of the top-hatted auctioneer gave out descriptions and registered bids from his pulpit-like rostrum. Early in the afternoon the hunt horses, who were the star turn in the catalogue, clopped in and out, reminding me—each one of them—of days that were no more. Toward the end of the sale my good-looking chestnut ' Crusader ' came under the hammer, and I regretfully saw that broken-winded but brilliant performer knocked down for about half what I'd given for him there exactly a year ago. He was bought by a Belgian cavalry officer, who was intending to make a show-jumper of him—an intention which was no doubt frustrated by the subsequent invasion of Belgium. Anyhow Norman had a highly satisfactory sale, and even the second whip's horses fetched their full value. Last on the list was the ugliest of the lot, a dejected-looking dun gelding called Kangaroo, whose knees I had chipped early in the season when jumping into a lane outside Twycross Wood. But even poor old Kangaroo found a buyer at twenty-seven guineas.

It had been so like revisiting a separate existence that while walking away from Tattersall's I may have wondered why it was so impossible to amalgamate my contrasted worlds of Literature and Sport. Why must I always be adapting my manners—and even my style of speaking—to different sets of people? Was it really necessary to exclude one world in order to find diversity in the other? Couldn't one contrive to combine them in 'one grand sweet song'? There were moments when I felt that I was an indecisive intruder who had no genuine foothold in either of those apparently incompatible spheres of activity. This problem—if I got as far as formulating it clearly—might have been solved for me by the personality of at least one living poet, probably the only one of any distinction who wouldn't have been totally out of his element at Tattersall's. This was Ralph Hodgson, whose magnificent lyrical poem *The*

*Song of Honour* had become famous since the previous year, when it had appeared in one of the little yellow chap-books which Lovat Fraser decorated so delightfully. Hodgson—though I was still unaware of it—might safely have been introduced to the most hard-boiled of my Atherstone acquaintances, could have taken any of them on at billiards, and given them plenty of first-hand information about the science of boxing. Also, though no lover of blood-sports, he had behind him a creditable career as a judge of bull-terriers at Cruft's Show and elsewhere—was in fact freely accepted as 'Mr. 'Odson' by many a tough sportsman who had never read a line of poetry in his life, and only knew verse through the medium of the music-hall song. However, had Hodgson decided to talk to them about poetry, I can almost believe that two or three—or even more—of the Atherstone Hunt Committee would have listened to him with respectful though not pellucid interest in his eloquence. He would probably have led up to the subject by starting a discussion on birds; for no-one knew the habits of a hawfinch better than he did.

Having ascertained from Eddie Marsh that Hodgson didn't look in the least like a poet and always went about in a bowler hat with a pipe in his mouth, I somehow sensed the fact that he was the man for my money, asked for his address, and was given a number in King's Road, Chelsea. To Chelsea I went, one soaking wet afternoon early in June, much hoping that I was about to meet the man who had written *The Song of Honour*. For there was a startling freshness in his poetic voice which had made his words come to life on the printed page in a way which I welcomed without being able to tell myself how the mystery was effected. I was eager to see what he was like, but I also wanted to thank him for what he had done. Nothing came of it, however. My repeated raps with the door-knocker awoke no response from the plain-faced little house where the poet was lodging. Having failed once I never went there again. The next two months passed without my being reminded of him by anyone, and I allowed diffidence to defeat my intuition that he was the sort of man I should get on well with. So we had to wait another five years before beginning our friendship.

Walking home damp and disappointed, I was anyhow spared the knowledge of how badly the haphazardness of Time was treating me. For had Hodgson been there to open the door I should have gained admittance to his many-sided and imaginative mind.

All that summer I was accompanied by a feeling —not unconnected with the physical richness of youth—that I was on the verge of some experience which might liberate me from my blind alley of excessive sport and self-imposed artistic solitude. I know now that a few evenings with Hodgson at Raymond Buildings would have made all the difference. He would have set my mind alight and put me on the right road to understanding myself, as he afterwards did, not by offering advice but by saying things which simplified one's problems and set one a standard.

Having mentioned 'the physical richness of youth', I am conscious that while writing this chapter I have somehow failed to communicate the feeling—so elusive when one attempts to express it—which haunts my memories of the time I spent at Raymond Buildings. It now seems to have been no more than this, that I was beginning to enjoy being about in London. I had grown up looking on it as a place whose grime and noisiness made one doubly thankful for living in the country. But there came a moment during that summer when I realized that I was acquiring a liking for its back-street smells and busy disregard of my existence. Walking home at night I began to be quite fond of Holborn, and I became aimlessly attached to certain places merely through passing them so often. I was learning to love the city breezes; the country thoughts they carried with them gave the town intensity, and taught one the value of its trees. The skies had never meant so much to me as they now did in dingy London. Sunsets beyond those roofs and chimneys, those miles of brick and mortar, affected me with a newly-discovered emotion, inexpressible and alluring with the vague regrets of my ignorant 'twenties. There was a sort of poetry behind it all which fed my mind and created stirrings of expectation.

## XIV

One afternoon in the second week of June I was going into Gray's Inn by the Holborn entrance. It was about five o'clock; the weather was sultry; and I was tired and in want of my tea. I was returning from a joyless expedition to an office in Old Broad Street, where I had made ineffectual efforts to induce our sympathetic but inflexible family solicitor to 'let me have an extra hundred pounds this quarter'. I had made no secret of the fact that the money was needed for the rent and renovation of my flat. 'But why—in your present embarrassed circumstances—take a flat at all, my dear boy?' the lawyer had inquired in his charmingly urbane voice. 'Had you never heard of such a thing as furnished rooms by the month?' He had added the inevitable truism about cutting one's coat according to one's cloth. I had replied that I hadn't thought about it at the time and had liked the idea of living in Gray's Inn. He agreed that there was nothing to be said against Gray's Inn, though he would have preferred me to be settled there with the object of reading for the Bar, which he regarded as a suitable basis for a literary career. I was therefore feeling somewhat down in the mouth and wondering how I was going to exist on next to nothing for the rest of the year. It was at this moment that I became aware of a fair-haired hatless young man who had passed me and was swinging along in the direction of Raymond Buildings. Something unusual about him drew my attention. He looked so self-contained and care-free as he went along the wide paved walk under the plane trees. Mending my pace, I saw him turn in at the doorway of Number Five, and this made me fairly certain who he was; for Eddie Marsh had told me quite lately that Rupert Brooke had sailed from New York, after a year's absence from England, and would soon be coming to stay with him.

So I've really seen the wonderful Rupert at last, I thought, while climbing rather wearily to my rooms. Somehow or other he had made me feel a bit of a failure.

Next day, however, kind Eddie sent me a note —'Come to breakfast to-morrow and meet Rupert and W. H. Davies'. I was agog with excitement, and it seemed almost too much for me to take in all at once! I was of course eager to know Davies, but Brooke was my exact contemporary, and the success of his poems had aroused in me an admiring antagonism stronger than anything I could feel about the admirable Nature Poet. The unromantic and provocative character of Brooke's 1911 volume had produced a vividly disturbing effect on my mind. Slow to recognize its abundant graces, I was prevented—by my prejudice against what I designated 'modern ugliness'—from perceiving his lovely and never prettified work as it really was. But in those days I didn't read things carefully or bend my mind to meanings. My unagile intellect was confused by his metaphysical cleverness. Interested though I was by the prospect of meeting the much-discussed young poet, I was unprepared to find him more than moderately likeable. Eddie's adoring enthusiasm had put me somehow on the defensive. In fact I had so far been quite unintelligent about Rupert Brooke, as the following anecdote against myself will testify.

One day toward the end of February, 1914, I was lunching with Eddie at the Ship Restaurant in Whitehall—a favourite rendezvous of his, owing to its being so near the Admiralty. During the meal he produced from an inner pocket a typewritten sheet from which he read me Brooke's as yet unpublished lines called *Heaven*.

> Fish (fly-replete in depth of June,
> Dawdling away their wat'ry noon) . . .

he began, while I listened—with what I now imagine to have been a rather fox-hunting face, since the reading aloud of poetry always makes me feel a bit shy and uncomfortable. As he proceeded toward its effective climax I can hardly have failed to realize that *Heaven* was amusing, though unconscious that it was a sensitive imitation of Andrew Marvell. But uppermost in the pond-like opacity of my brain was the fact that Brooke had also written *The Fish*, one of the finest poems he ever wrote. So when Eddie proclaimed, with enchanted finality,

> And in that Heaven of all their wish
> There shall be no more land, say fish . . .

my—alas—unhesitating valuation of one of the most magically witty poems in the language was merely ' Why does he always write about fishes? ' This must have been about the blankest crudity I ever inflicted on ever-lenient Eddie, who thereupon dropped his eye-glass and protested, with agonized intensity.

' But my dear, he *doesn't!* And the only other fish poem he wrote isn't in the *least* like this one! '

That much I was obliged to admit; and he went on to say that he simply *couldn't* understand why a certain Literary Editress had rejected *Heaven* on the ground that it was too audaciously outspoken for the general public. Not only incomprehensible but incredible seems that rejection now, when the literary public accepts the unprintable as being all in the day's work.

* * *

Breakfast was already well under way when I became aware that Rupert Brooke had entered the room. He had slipped in unnoticed, for the door was behind me and my attention was being held by Davies, whose eyes had an expression of child-like nobility. I looked up, and he was at my elbow, composedly awaiting the jubilant 'Welcome home from foreign parts!' with which his friend Davies greeted him. Eddie then introduced me to him; he shook hands rather shyly. From the first I got the impression that the great Rupert Brooke was quite a modest chap after all.

At this date it is perhaps unnecessary to describe what he looked like. He was wearing an open-necked blue shirt and old grey flannel trousers, with sandals on bare feet, and hadn't bothered to brush his brown-gold hair, which was, I thought, just a shade longer than it need have been. Seen in the full light as he sat beside the window, his eyes were a living blue and his face was still sunburnt from outdoor life on a

Pacific Island. He seemed much less wide-awake than Davies, who had walked all the way from Bloomsbury, and during most of the meal he remained rather aloof and uncommunicative. This was excusable, since he had probably been up late the night before, and in addition to that the kidneys and bacon cooked by admirable Mrs. Elgy were something he may well have sighed for from the South Seas. But with honey on his toast he brightened up, exchanging a joke or two with Eddie and listening with grave amusement to the discoursings of Davies, who was relating—at some length—a not wildly interesting experience he'd once had on the banks of the Mississippi.

Davies, by the way, was delightfully avuncular when talking to the younger poets, toward whom his attitude was pardonably patronizing. He was a simple unspeculative man, richly seasoned with genuine shrewdness which served him well as long as he applied it to what he understood. Beyond that his natural wisdom failed him, and he sometimes misjudged men and their motives with artless vanity and intolerance. But the social simplicity of ' Little Bill ' is best exemplified by the engaging story of him replying ' Some of the neighbours, I suppose ' when asked who had been present at a reading of his poetry which he had given to a drawing-room full of fashionable and artistic celebrities. The personal charm of Davies, however, was the abundant happiness and contentment which is so beautifully apparent in his imperishable poetry.

But I am digressing from my reminiscence of Rupert Brooke, whom I had been observing evasively, wondering the while how it was that he struck me as being so unlike what I had expected. My glimpse of him a couple of days before had been nearer my preconceived notion, for he had been neatly dressed in conventional clothes and had looked, if anything, a little over-satisfied with himself. Was it his way of speaking which now seemed vaguely associated with something in my own experience? Groping for the clue, I got it at last. Absurdly enough, it was nothing more than the word *Cambridge*. Why had I forgotten to connect him with Cambridge, when there was that brilliant Grantchester poem of his which I knew so well? I had known too that he'd gone up to King's in my last term at Clare, and had sometimes wondered how often I'd walked past him in the street. Anyhow, wasn't he still rather the same sort of highly intelligent young man my brother Hamo used to go rock-climbing with in Wales before he went to his engineering job in the Argentine? And those *sandals* (were they Tahitan, I wondered), didn't they somehow suggest certain young men—and young women also—of whom my mother was wont to remark that she did wish they wouldn't dress in that sloppily artistic way and talk silly Fabian Socialism? . . . At the present moment, however, I felt that I myself had reacted against that kind of thing too much—by trying to become a hard-boiled sportsman, dressing the part, and getting the name of my London club put on my visiting-card. Brooke had obviously done better by being a Cambridge intellectual and suppressing the fact that he'd played cricket and football for Rugby. The difference between us seemed to be that his idea of adventure was to go half across the world and write vividly about it, while mine was to go somewhere in Warwickshire, gallop after a pack of hounds, and stop being a writer altogether!

Breakfast being now at an end, 'Bill' Davies lit his bull-dog pipe and settled down to discuss poetry with the others. But it was the business side of poetry which he talked about, and this made me feel rather out of it, since the sales of *Georgian Poetry*—already in its tenth thousand—and the market for verse among literary editors were subjects in which I had as yet no professional concern. I should have liked to hear them exchanging ideas on poetry as an art, but it was too early in the day for that sort of thing. Had it been ten o'clock in the evening they would probably have said much that was worth listening to, and I might have heard how to make words obedient—how to catch imaginations on the wing and control them in rhythms and rhymes.

Meanwhile the time had arrived when E. Marsh, C.M.G., must betake himself to his duties at the Admiralty. Could it be possible that Eddie—now finishing a supplementary half-cup of that delicious China tea and telling me not to hurry away from the poets unless I had something else to do—would in a brace of shakes be in close attendance on Mr. Winston Churchill, and quite conceivably popping round to the Prime Minister on some private-secretarial errand appertaining to the Navy? Anyhow, off he went—to reappear for a moment with bowler hat and umbrella and administer a quick final injunction to Rupert—'Don't forget we're lunching with Lady Horner to meet Mr. Birrell, and *do* try to be in time!'

As I said before, Eddie's share in the activities of Cabinet Ministers was a thing which I regarded with almost obsequious reverence. I looked upon him as the sealed receptacle of political secrets which would never get into the newspapers—or even into the future volumes of English History! . . . This reminds me that my own contact with Cabinet Ministers had so far been restricted to a single incident in my boyhood. Under a temporarily-erected awning in the Strand, during the unveiling of my Uncle Hamo's statue of the late Mr. Gladstone, I had touched the elbow of the Duke of Devonshire with the tip of my fore-finger. I had been respectfully surprised by observing that the Duke's overcoat (he was an absent-minded-looking old buffer with an auburn-grey beard) was positively shabby, especially at the back of its blue velvet collar. But I felt that it might bring me luck in life if I touched him; so after he'd made a long slow speech and pulled the unveiling cord, I edged up behind him in the crowd and did it. Of Mr. Gladstone, by the way, I knew almost nothing beyond the fact that he had—no one could tell me why—taken the head of the table at my Aunt Rachel's wedding breakfast. I had also heard that he chewed every mouthful eighty times, and as a child I used to wonder whether he did so while consuming his slice of Auntie Rachel's wedding-cake.

★ ★ ★

Soon afterwards Davies departed, and I was alone with Rupert Brooke for about half-an-hour. Some way removed from me, he sat by a window serenely observing the trees of Gray's Inn gardens. From time to time his eyes met mine, but it was with a clouded though direct regard. I was conscious that his even-toned voice was tolerant rather than communicative, and that his manner had become gravely submissive to the continuing presence of a stranger. He may have been shy, but I am afraid he was also a little bored with me. We agreed that Davies was an excellent poet and a most likeable man. I then asked him a few clumsy questions about his travels. His replies were reserved and unilluminating. One fragment of our talk which I remember clearly was—as such recoveries often are—wholly to my disadvantage.

'What were the white people like in the places you stayed at in the tropics?' I had asked. ('The tropics' sounded somehow inept, but it was too late to correct myself now!)

'Some of them', he said, 'were rather like composite characters out of Conrad and Kipling.'

Hoping that it would go down well, I made a disparaging remark about Kipling's poetry being terribly tub-thumping stuff.

'But not always, surely,' he answered; and then let me off easily by adding, 'I used to think rather the same myself until Eddie made me read *Cities and Thrones and Powers*. There aren't many better modern poems than that, you know.'

I could only admit that I had never read it.

And yet, if I'd been more at my ease, I might have saved my credit by telling him that I knew by heart the first eight lines, which I really loved, of Kipling's ' Neither the harps nor the crowns amused, nor the cherubs' dove-winged races '.

After that it seemed safer not to mention poetry any more. It would be comforting if I could record that I expressed some admiration for his work—if I had said, for instance, how delightful I thought his Grantchester poem. But I didn't. I was, indeed, reduced to informing him of the uninspiring fact that we'd been at Cambridge together for a term—the autumn one of 1906. Yes, that was his first term there, he replied, and he'd acted in the Greek play—the *Eumenides* it was—as the Herald. This was something I'd entirely forgotten, though it came back to me vividly now. For the Herald had been such a striking figure that everybody in Cambridge had talked about him. But I didn't mystify him by exclaiming ' So I *had* seen you before! ' I merely thought how odd it was that I had never connected the Herald in his gorgeous red and gold with the young poet whose work had since then startled and attracted me.

Meanwhile I was only one more in the procession of people who were more interested in him than he was in them. For after all, why should he be interested in me, much though I now wanted to know him better? To him I was merely an amateur poet who had scarcely arrived at publication, strongly flavoured with the Philistinism of the hunting field. His intellectual development was years ahead of me, and his character was much more fully formed than mine. I was still slowly unlearning the mental immaturities which he had got rid of before he was twenty-one. From me, as I then was, he could have acquired nothing. So there we were, and my present notion is that I felt rather like a Lower Fifth Form boy talking to the Head of the School!

During that singular encounter it was his kindness, I think, which impressed me, and the almost meditative deliberation of his voice. His movements, too, so restful, so controlled, and so unaffected. But beyond that was my assured perception that I was in the presence of one on whom had been conferred all the invisible attributes of a poet. To this his radiant good looks seemed subsidiary. Here, I might well have thought—had my divinations been expressible—was a being singled out for some transplendent performance, some enshrined achievement. That, I believe, was the effect he made on many of those who met him as I did, and on all who fully understood the strength and sweetness of his nature.

Anyhow, there he was, aloof in his unforeseeingness of what was to come after, just a little weary of me, but all beautifully polite while he waited for me to go away. And here was I, regretfully aware that I had failed to interest him and was using up more of his morning than he could afford to spare me. There is no need to explain that our one brief meeting had a quite unpredictable significance. Nor need I underline the latent irony of the situation. When bidding me good-bye at Eddie's outer door his demeanour implied that as far as he was concerned there was no apparent reason why we should ever meet again. He may even have breathed a sigh of relief at having got rid of me at last, as he closed the door quietly and went back to being his unimpeded self.

## XV

When I returned to my rooms I became dejectedly aware of the fact that I had nothing to do for the rest of the day. I felt that Eddie's breakfast party ought to have been given in the evening. Eleven o'clock in the morning was the wrong time to come home from a festive gathering. My half-furnished rooms looked lonely, and seemed to be wondering why I was back again so soon on such a fine day, and I couldn't help wishing that I was in a hurry to catch a train to some pleasant house in the country, preferably a large one in the middle of an ancient deer-park. As no such place awaited my arrival, I decided that the only thing to do was to go for a meditative walk in Regent's Park. Having betaken myself there, and finding myself in the vicinity of the Zoological Gardens, it struck me that as I hadn't been there since I was about ten years old I might as well wander in. It would anyhow be more animated than the British Museum!

But the Zoo proved unenlivening. It made me feel more solitary than ever, and its inhabitants appeared to be filling-in time as listlessly as I was. I began badly with the eagles and vultures, though

I took it that the motionless morosity with which they ignored me was nothing unusual. A browsing buffalo seemed to have a vague resemblance to some unamiable person I had known, but I couldn't make out who it was. The lions, tigers, and leopards were in an abstracted doze or else prowling restlessly up and down their cages, while the non-carnivorous animals were munching mechanically as though resigned to certainty that nothing unexpected could ever occur to them again. A monkey looked at me as if he, at any rate, had something he would like to tell me, and then sighed and looked away, wondering why either of us was there. The penguins were feeling disheartened by the mid-day heat. Nothing seemed to be in its proper element except the seals and sea-lions, who were wallowing contentedly in their water.

Hot and jaded, I sat down and closed my eyes, listening to the queer mixture of squawks, chatterings, and ululations by which the place was pervaded. A tree screened me from the sun, and some little birds were twittering and whistling in an aviary near by. A few minutes' rest would perhaps put me in the mood for a museful investigation of the reptile house. Not far from my seat there was a raven who had a roomy cage to himself. When I opened my eyes a few minutes later

I observed a small and somewhat oddly dressed old lady who had her back to me and was addressing confidential remarks to the raven. He was apparently receiving them with approval. I waited until she turned to move slowly on, since I didn't want to startle her, and she had seemed completely unconscious of her surroundings while confabulating with the bird. It had not taken me many moments to realize that this was my old friend Wirgie.

Her manner of greeting me silently implied everything that was in both our minds and might have been said by her. For the fact was that although I'd written in April to tell her about my flat in Gray's Inn I had—for some unexplainable reason—failed to communicate with her since I came to London. She expressed her awareness of all this by gazing intently up at my face with an unreproachful solemnity which somehow emanated from her closed lips, as though they were a part of her countenance that embarrassed and yet amused her. It was a look which made further explanations unnecessary. We were glad to see one another again, and she had no intention of being offended with me, though I knew that I deserved it. Anyhow the Zoo was a very good place for being with Wirgie, and my dull-mindedness vanished immediately. Having introduced me to the raven, whose name was Rab, she conducted me to many of her favourites, some of whom I had already inspected with apathetic eyes. ' I know all their personal habits intimately ', she remarked, and it was evident that she was on friendly terms with the men who looked after them, for she was one of those lonely people who spend many hours in museums and public galleries, conversing with the attendants and sometimes exchanging ideas with casual strangers. At the Zoo she humanized everything in an almost mysterious way, owing to her imaginative sympathy for anything from a lion to a lizard. She confessed however that she had so far found the rhinoceros unresponsive, adding that although she came there so often she was made unhappy by seeing all these intensely active creatures in unnatural captivity. ' The Zoo isn't at all a civilized institution, you know ', she said. ' Very few of these animals enjoy being protected from one another. And most of them have much more dignity than the people who come here to gape at them.'

Later on, when we were lunching off poached eggs and tinned peaches, it became necessary for me to tell her something of my activities in London. In fact she invited me to do so, though all she said was ' Well? . . .' which somehow conveyed that I needn't divulge more than I wanted to. I was, of course, unable to admit that my time in town had thus far been a failure, so I made the best of it by restricting my disclosures to the breakfast party, allowing her to assume that it was merely the most recent of many interesting experiences among authors, and that this visit to the Zoo was a quiet interlude in my concatenation of social engagements. Like most young people, I often made fun of my own dilemmas in a self-deprecating way, but my loneliness in London wasn't a thing I could treat facetiously. After remarking that my Mr. Marsh seemed to go in for keeping a positive aviary of poets, she inquired eagerly about W. H. Davies, and reminded me of our delighted discovery of him about seven years before. I was able to tell her that he wasn't at all unlike his poems, and she quoted some lines where he describes a swallow cutting the name of summer in the clear blue air. A swallow's flight was so exactly like someone skating gracefully, she said, and the word summer, when one came to think of it, was a series of curves as one wrote it. Realizing that I myself had been unaware that the skating metaphor was there at all, and thinking what a percipient judge of poetry she was, I watched her produce a very brown banana from that old bag of hers, the cryptic and long-accumulated contents of which were a well-worn joke of ours.

After inspecting the banana she musefully decided to keep it for one of the monkeys. But she was beginning to look tired, so I said good-bye, after she had promised to go to a concert with me quite soon. Any afternoon or evening would find her free, she said, if I could fit it into my whirligig of gaieties!

*     *     *

Wirgie had so successfully stimulated my interest in the Zoo that early on the following afternoon I went there again. It had occurred to me also that I might be able to write a piece of semi-satirical verse about it, somewhat in the manner of Rupert Brooke, so I was in a pleasantly purposeful frame of mind, though my observations led to nothing more than a sonnet in which I described my recognition of two of my sporting acquaintances in the Chimpanzee and the Orang-outang. Meanwhile the weather was even warmer than it had been the day before, and I was strolling placidly towards the sea-lions' pool. The one idea which hadn't crossed my mind was that Wirgie might likewise have decided to go there again, so I felt rather disconcerted and ridiculous when I saw her advancing in my direction. About fifty yards of asphalt path lay between us, and while we slowly converged her demeanour expressed apologetic hesitancy, as though she ought to pretend not to see me. For although I hadn't actually pretended that I was leading a busy life, I had given her no cause for expecting to find me loafing about at the Zoo two days running! Here I was again, however, quite obviously with nothing else to do, and her sense of the situation showed itself, as she took my hand, in a mutely eloquent look of amused humility, followed by a low gurgling laugh. After which there was nothing to prevent a repetition of our conversational saunterings as though they had never been interrupted. And as before, she gave the whole place a sense of strangeness—a sense of intimacy with the beasts and birds and the far foreign distances to which they belonged. But when I asked her to come back to Raymond Buildings and have tea with me she firmly refused. She was much too unpresentable, she said. It would impair my social position if I were seen entering Gray's Inn with such a dowdy satellite. A few days later, however, we went to an afternoon concert, and as she was now looking quite 'the duchess' she was easily persuaded to come and inspect my 'swell establishment'. At the concert we heard the first London performance of a long quartet by Schönberg, whose works were at that time being received with mystified curiosity and hostility. We could make nothing of it, and

I remember how amused she was when a rising young musical critic, who happened to be sitting just behind us, summarized the new work as 'rather Schumannesque'. 'Rather caterwaulesque!' was her own *sotto-voce* comment; for the soprano solo in the final movement certainly had seemed excruciatingly antagonistic to its accompaniment, though it would probably sound quite ordinary if one listened to it now.

Afterwards, when I was piloting her up the stairway to my rooms, I may have thought of the place where she herself had lived alone for many years. I had never been asked to enter it, for she was sensitive on the subject, but I suspected that it was rather cheerless and uncomfortable. I knew that her flat was somewhere at the top of a tall dreary building half-way up Campden Hill, for I had been there once, to leave a propitiatory bunch of flowers when she had been offended with me through my failure to keep an appointment. (Wirgie, however brief the duration of her displeasure, was always 'deeply offended'.) It seemed probable that she existed in a state of considerable untidiness. But the smallness of her income made her unapproachably proud, and it would have been a bad day for any friend who ventured to inquire how much she'd got per annum. She had, however, told me a lot about the cat who was her sole companion, and at one time there had been references to a highly intelligent hare, which ended in being too sad a subject to be mentioned.

'I never thought to find you living in affluence among lawyers!' she exclaimed, as we passed two doorways with multiple and legal-looking names above them. I was able to inform her that Dickens had been employed in one of these very offices as a young man, thus conferring an associative immortality on the twisting stone steps which we were slowly ascending. For a moment she paused to think about it. 'What a world he must have carried about with him in that marvellous head!' she remarked, adding that he was always in love with his writing when he remembered places like this and the queer people who went in and out of them. On entering the flat her eye was at once attracted by my top-hat, which was glossily reposing on a small table in the entrance hall. This—and my neatly-rolled umbrella, solitary in its stand—she looked at with a sort of serious amusement. 'Are they symbolic of your social position?' she asked. But I now fancy that she saw something vaguely pathetic in the newness and simplicity of the place and the way my few belongings were so carefully arranged.

Meanwhile the tea-table was all set out, and

while I was boiling the water she inspected and admired what she called my positively palatial abode. She was the first person I had entertained there, which made me feel that I had something to preen myself about. Remembering that peacock-blue room in the past, apparently so propitious and inaugural, with its windows open to the June sunshine and the whispering full-foliaged trees, I find Wirgie talking just a little more whimsically than she need have done, as though conscious that I had outgrown the ingenuous youth for whom she used to 'do Godowsky giving a quiet encore'. At the Zoo we had been our old selves, she in her untidy clothes and I meeting her on her own ground with spontaneous impulsiveness. But here, in these emancipative surroundings of mine, she may have had a prevision of what must have happened to her with many of her young friends, whom time had carried into highways of experience where their intuitive association with her was remembered only in a passing pang of self-reproach for having lost sight of her. The confiding and receptive young creatures came and went; and she enjoyed her intimacy with them while it lasted. She could have told me how life imposes its laws of change and recurrence; but I should not have understood, though I dimly guessed what it meant to be old and poor and lonely. For the present she was doing her best to 'be the duchess' and playing at quizzical astonishment that I had emerged from what I'd been when she last saw me. We were both of us however a little fatigued by having listened to so much exactingly modern music; and there was quite a chance that we might become involved in one of those misunderstandings which could reduce conversation to a somewhat sultry silence.

'You've been coming on quite terrifically since I gleamed my accomplished eye over you last year, haven't you?' she remarked, settling herself in a corner of my luxurious sofa with a cup of perfumed China tea in her hand. I replied that I didn't feel as if I'd made as much progress as all that. Hunting in Warwickshire hadn't got me anywhere, and it didn't seem as if writing poetry would get me anywhere either. 'What exactly do you mean by that, young sir?' she inquired. An access of moody dissatisfaction caused me to assert that I'd given up believing that I'd got anything to write about. She answered me with the following anecdote.

'Years ago, a rather lively young novelist earnestly assured me that he felt completely finished. About eighteen months afterwards he had a huge success with a slightly improper book, and was very soon dining at all the smart houses where poor old Wirgie never gets invited at all. Next time we met by accident in Kensington Gardens I reminded him of what he'd said. And some fine day I shall do the same to you! ' she concluded, gazing intently at Titian's serious-eyed young man over the mantelpiece and wondering aloud whether he ever guessed how well known in the world his features would become.

She had already put her finger on the main deficiency of my rooms by saying that I ought never to be without a piano. For it was true that my mind had often felt musicless and in need of the emotionally enrichening companionship of my piano. Its presence would have made all the difference to us at that particular moment; she would have played to me for a few minutes and our minds would have been at rest. As it was she fell back on tâlking about the old days when we did so much ' Debussying ' together, and how midsummery my mother's garden had been while we sat out of doors after dinner. But I wasn't in the mood for such retrospections, and was unwilling to be reminded of that period a few years ago when my day-dreams had been so alive with poetic promise. Before long I reverted to my present day problems and indulged in another outburst of self-depreciation. What, I asked, was the use of expecting oneself to do anything wonderful or even to develop into anything very different from the sort of person one was now? I cannot recall the actual remark which finally reduced poor Wirgie to dejection, but whatever it was my undiverting utterance caused her to give me one of those mutely regretful looks which signified that I had said something recklessly rudimentary and that she was forbearingly permitting it to pass unrebuked. Realizing that I had provoked a situation which needed recovering from, I took the tea-things into the kitchen and remained there for nearly ten minutes washing-up and putting everything away with time-filling thoroughness. While thus occupied I could hear Wirgie soliloquizing in urgent undertones. It reminded me of the way she had talked to the raven. But with him she had been calm and confidential; he had said nothing to wound her feelings as I, apparently, had done. I wondered why she should be so upset by my saying that nothing ever changes enough to make any real difference. It did not occur to me that life, with its failures and frustrations, had taught her more than she needed to know about mutability. I only knew that she was addressing a mournful expostulation against something I had said without considering its effect. What that effect was I am now able to imagine. I can infer from that then half-audible monologue that she was testifying—to an unheeding audience of her vanished selves—the inexpressible futility of explaining to the young those things which they will never find out until they have discovered the truth by knocking their heads against it. And after that I see her sitting alone and silent; alone with her inscrutable cognizance and understanding, in comparison with which I knew no more about life than a sparrow in Gray's Inn gardens. Or is she merely feeling as old as the hills, while the westering sun looks in at my blue-walled room and I am wiping the cups and saucers in the kitchen?

When I rejoined her she said no more about our misunderstanding, and soon afterwards I saw her step safely into an omnibus, which she did with absent-minded unhurrying dignity. Next day I received a post-card from her. 'Someone—I can't remember who—said that we see clearly a second time through the spectacles of experience. My own experience is that half one's life is spent in trying to understand things and the other half in trying to make other people understand what one has learnt. I could add other aphorisms, but remain yrs affecy H.W.' The wisdom of this message was wasted on me. I merely thought how unlike anyone else's her upright handwriting was—and how inseparable from her speaking self.

It had the distinctness of a musical manuscript, the firm delicacy of a sensitive drawing, and the fluency of her richly-remembering mind.

* * *

Although I had declared to Wirgie that there was no probability of my developing into anything much unlike what I then was, it did at any rate seem fairly certain that my three years' lease of those rooms in Raymond Buildings meant that I should still be going up and down the stairs in three years' time. I should have been incredulous had I been told that after July, 1914, I should only use the rooms for a few days in the spring of the following year. What followed might have perplexed me even more. In the subsequent years I did occasionally go into Gray's Inn, but it was not until the autumn of 1941 that I again climbed the stairs to my former flat. I then discovered that mutability had done its work with Germanic thoroughness. The solid outer door remained, but the interior had vanished. My top-floor rooms were the only part of Raymond Buildings which had been completely destroyed. So I came away feeling that there wasn't much more to be said about them. . . . Pottering sadly around Gray's Inn gardens I picked up a much damaged but decipherable legal document—one of many which were lying about among the ruins of burnt-out offices. I was surprised to find that it referred to the will of a man named Sparrow; for I had already written the passage in which I have compared myself to one of those birds. Why that name, of all others? I wondered.

# XVI

At about six o'clock one perfect midsummer afternoon I was strolling up St. James's Street, agreeably conscious that I was wearing my smartest clothes and that my top-hat had come into its own again. For the moment I felt quite a man about town, though my plunge into social dissipation had been a blamelessly well-behaved one. After a light but discriminative lunch at a fashionably quiet restaurant in Jermyn Street I had conducted my great-aunt to a matinée of a politely sensational but undistinguished drawing-room drama called *My Lady's Dress*. My great-aunt had bought me a dark-red carnation for my buttonhole; and this was now contributing to the jauntiness of my mental demeanour.

My great-aunt Mozelle, I must hasten to explain, was neither antiquated nor frumpy. My great-grandfather had died fifty years before, but she had been only eight years old then. Elegant, lively, and charming, she was still in the prime of life, and none of her numerous nephews and great-nephews could fail to feel gratified by being seen with her. She was also one of the few members of my father's family with whom I could claim to be on even top-hat-raising terms. (I had sometimes thought that my social position would be stronger if I were acquainted with a few more of them—in Park Lane and elsewhere.)

Aunt Mozelle had known my father well and still spoke of him with affection. In my childhood I had seen her occasionally at my aunt Rachel's house, but there had been an interval of nearly fifteen years, and even then we had met again by the merest accident. It was an episode which she frequently recalled with enjoyment, and this very afternoon she had reminded me—in that pleasant faintly foreign voice of hers—how I had recognized her at a lawn meet somewhere in Sussex and greeted her with the words 'Hullo, Aunt Brazil Nut!'—this being the inappropriate name which my brothers and I had formerly conferred on her. To commemorate the occasion she had subsequently presented me with a small silver box made in the shape of a brazil nut, and our happily renewed relationship had enabled me to acquire many details of my family history which might otherwise have been inaccessible to me. I had always wanted to know more about my great-grandfather, David Sassoon, whom my mother had encouraged me to venerate vaguely as a man of noble character and wonderful ability, though I had found it difficult to connect myself with an ancestor who couldn't speak English and dressed like a Biblical patriarch. Anyhow, he had been Aunt Mozelle's father, and she was the only person I was likely to meet who had known him when he was alive. I wished that she had been a few years older when she was with him, but the little she could tell me had made him much less mythical for me.

Apart from this I had gained a solid satisfaction from the fact that in her I had found a relation who could make the other members of my father's family seem less far-removed and fabulous. People had so often put me in a false position by assuming that I knew all the conspicuous Sassoons, and I had been unwilling to confess that I was only a sort of poor relation, compensated however by being half a Thornycroft in blood and more than that in hereditary characteristics.

In the meantime I had just bidden a fond good-bye to her outside Garland's Hotel, and was now—as I have already related—on my way up the gentle slope of St. James's Street, when whom should I encounter but my one time house-master, Mr. Gould! Someone had told me that he had retired a few years before and had become a regular frequenter of the Carlton Club, to which his activities as a pillar of the Tory Party in North Wilts had secured him election. Club life, however, didn't appear to be agreeing with his constitution, for his nose was more blue and bulbous than ever above his tobacco-stained moustache, and he looked so doddery that I felt that he would be all the better for country air and a few games of croquet, at which he had been such a reputed expert. But it was our first meeting since I had left Marlborough in 1904, and I felt quite pleased at seeing him. I also hoped that my much-matured and almost man-of-the-worldish exterior would impress him favourably. I therefore greeted him with the decorous jollity which I considered appropriate to the occasion. This caused him to pull up and focus me with a genial but somewhat alcoholic gaze. ' Hullo, you fellow ', he muttered; and then added—after a brief pause for inspiration—' Well, and are you still as silly as ever? ' After patting me on the arm he nodded amiably and toddled away, taking his usual very short steps, in the direction of Pall Mall and the evening papers.

Remembering that his final advice to me when I left Marlborough had been ' Try to be more sensible ', I was more amused than offended by his disrespectful attitude toward my career. For after all I had never shown him any sign of being the sort of person who might give him cause to be proud of me! Thanking my stars that I should never have to go back to his house, I went quickly on towards Gray's Inn, as though by increasing my pace I were making funny old Gould even more of a back number than—in my estimation—he already was. And while putting Shaftesbury Avenue and Soho behind me I wondered why it was that one's feet felt more consciously important when wearing white spats than when they weren't—a simple problem which has probably been pondered by more profound intellects than mine.

I had now reached what appeared to be the zenith of my London season. For I was hurrying home to boil myself a couple of eggs and thereafter to emerge in full evening dress to attend a Gala Performance of the Russian Ballet. I was justified in regarding it as something beyond a gala performance for me, because I had never been to the Ballet before, and although Russian Opera and Ballet had been going on at Drury Lane for some time, the names of Chaliapin and Diaghilev had somehow failed to impress me with their proper significance. My experience of grand opera had hitherto consisted in a single Carl Rosa performance of *Carmen* (to which I had been taken while on my way home from school for the Christmas holidays) and my quite recent expedition to hear *The Magic Flute*. And I must admit that my enjoyment of Mozart's music had been fatiguingly interfered with by inability to understand what the opera was all about, although it was being given in English.

Walking through Covent Garden Market late at night, with an appreciative nose for the smells of flowers and vegetables, I had seen the society crowd coming away from the Opera, but had felt that I shouldn't get much out of it owing to my ignorance of Italian. What the Russian Ballet would be like I had no notion, and the first person who said anything about it to me was Eddie Marsh, who happened to ask whether I'd been to *Schéhérazade* yet. I replied that I wasn't particularly keen about ballets because nothing much ever seemed to happen in them—an offhand assertion which, as I afterwards discovered, was peculiarly inapplicable to *Schéhérazade*. His pained and reproachful retort—'But it's simply the most divine thing in the world!' had given me the needed stimulus, and I'd made a start by securing a central stall for the London première of *The Legend of Joseph*. This I obtained by luck—the box-office chancing to have a returned ticket when all the seats had been sold. Richard Strauss, who had written the music, was to conduct, and a youthful dancer named Léonide Massine would be making his début.

So when I at last set out for Drury Lane it seemed that I was anyhow doing the thing in good style. Making my way into the theatre, however, my sense of inexperience, as I left the daylight behind, amounted almost to nervousness! This feeling was intensified when I found myself wedged in the loquacious crowd which congested the approaches to the auditorium. It was rather as if I had arrived uninvited at an enormous but exclusive party. Borne along by the ingoing tide of ticket-holders, I seemed to be surrounded by large smiling ladies with bejewelled bosoms who looked like retired prima-donnas and whose ample presences were cavaliered by suave grey-haired men who might possibly be successful impresarios. They all seemed to know one another, and none of them appeared to mind whether everyone else heard what they were saying. Thus I continued confusedly impressed until I was safe in my seat, submerged in the buzzing excitement of a brilliant audience keyed-up to concert pitch for a memorable artistic event. It was indeed an occasion of almost international importance. Some people sitting behind me were talking German in loud and self-assertive voices, and there was a lot of bowing from one of the boxes which contained a man who looked as if he ought to be the German ambassador.

I hadn't troubled to provide myself with a programme, for I have always preferred to do my sight-seeing without a guide-book—an injudicious habit which once resulted in my approaching the Vatican without being aware of its identity. So I sat there fully expecting that when the curtain rose I should be witnessing *The Legend of Joseph*. The conductor was greeted with adequate applause, and I took it for granted that he was Strauss. After that I surrendered to a state of receptive mystification. I had been prepared to see the story of Joseph treated in an unusual way, but I was unable to make out how the opening scene could have any connexion at all with the Old Testament. A ballet, I assumed, wasn't compelled to conform closely to its subject matter, but no attempt had been made to orientalize anything. It wasn't even a Russian rendering of Jewish life in Egypt. These young ladies in conventional white ballet dresses had as their background the dark-foliaged avenue of a delightful old French château. And the yellow-haired young man with white silk legs and a short black velvet jacket who bounded about among them with such languishing and affected exuberance—could he really be intended for Joseph? Beautiful but bewildering it was; and the music sounded so familiar that I began to wonder whether Strauss had taken to imitating Chopin. (I looked rather than listened, and at that time I wasn't very good at identifying music in unfamiliar surroundings.) The only solution seemed to be that it was some sort of fantastic prelude. This, in a way, proved to be the explanation, for I was, of course, watching *Les Sylphides*.

During the interval I remained in my seat, and when the theatre was darkened again I felt assured that the event of the evening was at last materializing, for the reception of Richard Strauss, pink-faced and imperturbable, was not to be mistaken. My perplexities were now at an end. The behaviour of Potiphar's wife made it quite clear who she was, and Massine—a thin nervous boy who looked pathetically young—was immediately recognizable as Joseph. There is no need to describe the performance, which was, as I remember it now, excessively long drawn out and elaborate. It included a magnificent banquet which was the most sumptuous spectacle I had ever seen; and altogether I felt that I'd got rather more than a guinea's-worth of gorgeousness. The music made no impression on me, and it is possible that I unconsciously realized that *The Legend of Joseph*—as was generally admitted afterwards—had been rather a heavy affair—a grandiose failure, in fact. The date of its production subsequently suggested that Belshazzar's Feast would have been a more appropriate subject for everyone concerned. Many people must have looked back on that evening as 'epitomizing the end of an epoch'.

Eddie Marsh being the only person among the scintillating audience whom I had any likelihood of knowing, I now set out on a self-conscious cruise in quest of him. Before long I caught sight of him standing at the top of a flight of steps. He was in monocled conversation with a couple of brainy-looking young men in dowdy dinner-jackets, to whom I was introduced without quite grasping their names. While Eddie chatted amiably on—although with a somewhat wandering eye—I felt that his temporary associates were regarding me with disapproval. Their way of looking at me may have been merely intellectual curiosity, but it seemed to suggest that Aunt Mozelle's carnation had no business to be in my buttonhole and that I was altogether too much of a society swell. I was however favoured with an independent opinion of what I'd been seeing on the stage, for one of them—in that see-saw intonation which has since become known as 'the Bloomsbury voice'—replied, when I inquired what he thought of *The Legend of Joseph*, that the Strauss music had sounded to him quite *dreadfully* mechanical and the décor was *surely* Berlin-Veronese at its *most* meretricious. Wondering whether he was a musical critic who had got in for nothing, and suppressing an inclination to ask him whether he'd come there to enjoy himself, I duly assimilated the word 'daycore', which was new to me, and inwardly resolved not to be put off my private appreciation of the 'Veronese' element in the show. What he would have thought about me had he known of my boobyish dilemma during *Les Sylphides* was unthinkable! Eddie, on the other hand, would probably have found it deliciously amusing.

The performance ended exquisitely with *Papillons*, which sent me homeward charmed and exhilarated. There was no need to remind myself of my former stupidity in assuming that I should be bored by the Ballet. It was enough that I intended to go again as often as I could. Back at Raymond Buildings, with my evening toggery and tight shiny shoes discarded, my brown tea-pot and tin of biscuits on the table, and Schumann's music making an accompaniment to my thoughts, I made inconclusive attempts to summarize the evening's experiences.

Now that it was all over I couldn't help feeling a bit lonely, for on my way out of the theatre it had seemed as if everyone except me must be 'going on somewhere else'. In the foyer there had been a conspicuous group of young people—among whom I more or less recognized the most photographed society beauty of the year—and I had lingered for a few moments to observe them. Their voices had been rather insolently audible, and one of them had rapturously exclaimed that 'the party was sure to be marvellous fun and food'. Handsome and high-spirited, they had made me wish that I were going with them, even though they were behaving as if they'd bought the whole place. If I were a real rich Sassoon I should probably have been one of them, and should have talked to titled ladies in tiaras and bowed to ambassadors in boxes. But that in itself wasn't my idea of being somebody, for I hadn't found fashionable people particularly interesting to talk to when they were out hunting.

Anyhow the party was in full swing by now, and Eddie Marsh was certain to be there. If I were to lie awake long enough I should hear the tinkle of the bell at the porter's lodge down below announcing his return. What would it feel like, I wondered, to be mixed up with all those mundane and opulent figures on whom I had gazed with shy and constrained curiosity—to be, perhaps, a minor celebrity among them, since one had to be either rich or well-known to gain admittance to what was called the great world? On the whole, however, I decided that I was rather hostile to them. They were the sort of thing that proud and solitary poets savagely satirized, although Eddie Marsh would most likely disapprove of me if I described them as lifting worldly faces to a diamond star and patronizing the arts with shallow sophistication. He would explain that a good many of them were simply heavenly people if one knew them properly, adding that the arts would be in a pretty poor way without them and their diamond constellations. And what would *they* be without the arts? I should loftily reply. . . .

The excitement of the evening had evaporated, and speculation was dissolving into reverie. Only the memory of *Papillons* remained, haunting my head with gaiety and regretfulness. In Schumann's music I had always found the essence of romantic lyrical feeling. He went straight to one's heartstrings, especially in the accompaniments of some of his songs. On the final page of *Papillons* the clock struck six; and in the ballet the revellers were promenading home in couples, while Pierrot watched them, moon-struck and despondent in the summer morning light.

Twiddling my fading carnation as I sat by the writing-table, I thought how prosily methodical my dictionary looked, lying there beside the treatise on prosody which had repelled all my efforts to make mental headway with it. Was it really worth while to put one's poetic ambitions before everything else? A depressing disbelief in my own abilities invaded me. Moments of vision had been mine, but they had never been translated into achievement. They had merely been intimations of a power which, as it now seemed, would find no fulfilment. My determination to write in the grand style had dwindled to a few cadences in a minor key, and I had gradually arrived at my recent realization that I had nothing in me to write about. Wouldn't it be better to live one's poetry in pursuit of heedless happiness, surrendering to the dream-led intoxication of romantic adventure? To be in love with life wasn't enough, when one was perpetually doing it by oneself. I wanted to be youthful with the young, to be light-hearted before it was too late. Why couldn't life be less unlike the Russian Ballet, allowing me to liberate my emotions among people as beautifully volatile as the dancers, enchantingly impassioned playmates taking no heed of to-morrow, who would welcome me to their idyllic environment as a prodigy of genius and good looks? For the moment I saw myself as possessing affinities with the Pierrot in *Papillons*, forgetting that my career as a sporting character had to a considerable extent counterbalanced the dreamer and his preference for life reflected in a mirror, his allurement to the idea of an existence like the background of a

Praeraphaelite picture where it was forever afternoon, and time was standing still to the lulling rumble of a mill-wheel and the watery murmur of a weir.

Meanwhile my actual resemblance was nearer to Joseph in the Old Testament legend. Remembering myself as I then was, I am inclined to moralize on the contrast between simplicity and sophistication. For it is a somewhat solemn warning, when we contemplate the safeguarding ignorance of our immaturity. Solemn, because to have learnt a little more usually meant becoming more unwise in a worse way, since not all the wisdom of the world can defend us when we are abandoning the integrity of our acceptive innocence.

So it is possible that I was luckier than I knew in being where—and what—I was, while the last tram clanked along Theobald's Road and my future was being prepared for me. Somewhere in that London summer night a grand party was being given in honour of the famous and world-weary German composer to whose applause I had contributed my clapping. Better for youth to be falling asleep with a snatch of *Papillons* still dancing in his head than to be acquiring disillusionment in that dazzling limbo of the coldly clever, the self-seeking, and the faithless.

## XVII

The Russians were at Drury Lane until the end of the third week in July. Undeterred by a persistent heat-wave, I went there almost every night, and as long as their season continued could assure myself that I had at last discovered something worth doing in London. Having become an enthusiast for the Ballet, I was even more excited by the Russian Operas, partly through their picturesqueness, but mainly because of Chaliapin, whom I heard eleven times. His acting and singing were so natural that they seemed to be one thing; I could almost forget that he was acting at all, though the dramatic effect was incomparably magnificent. The gallery must have been one of the hottest places in London, but I gladly joined the queue and jostled up the narrow stairs to swelter among a crowd of exuberant foreigners and get a bird's-eye view of Boris Godounov in the ghost scene, or the wily and formidable Tartar Kontchak in his camp on the Steppes.

These operas were a romantic discovery which appealed to my imagination more than any dramatic performance I had hitherto experienced.

The fact that I couldn't understand a word of what the singers were saying and had hazy notions about the scenic developments only added to their thrill and mystery, though I found out a bit more when Wirgie accompanied me—as she twice did—to the front row of the Grand Circle, sharing my delight as no one else could have done.

In the daytime people were going about as usual; the grass in the parks was being burnt brown, and riders moved lazily in the shade along the Row; militant suffragettes were getting themselves arrested in public places, as I observed one afternoon from the top of a bus near Hyde Park Corner; the members of my club sat reading about 'The Ulster Question' in their newspapers with undiminished inertness. But my head was haunted by the half-oriental sadness of Russian music, the *sotto-voce* recitatives of Chaliapin, and the legendary poetic feeling of all that colour and movement which was nocturnally alluring me at Drury Lane. And the Russian Ballet had been going on during the two previous summers while I was feeling bored with myself in Kent and knowing nothing at all about it!

Back to Kent I now went, hugging the piano scores of *Prince Igor* and *Boris Godounov*, from which I hoped to derive consolation for the final fall of the curtain on my entrancements.

To be playing my way through the declamatory pages of Borodin and Moussorgsky did indeed provide pleasant emotional relaxation in the cool of the evening, and I found refuge from reality when the candles were alight on the piano and the summer scents of the garden were coming in through the open windows of the drawing-room. But at other times I was despondently digesting the fact that my financial condition compelled me to vegetate at home and spend next to nothing for an indefinite period. Playing the piano was about the only occupation I could afford to indulge in. Working it out on paper, I arrived at the dispiriting discovery that I needed five hundred pounds to put me straight, and had no prospect of obtaining even a fraction of that amount. This was more than enough to make me groan and scratch my head, but I had sufficient sense of proportion to realize that a quandary which could be surmounted by an improbable acquisition of five hundred quid need not be regarded as constituting a permanent blight on one's career. What seriously troubled me was my conviction that something really had gone wrong with that career of mine.

It was possible, I found, to divide myself—as I had existed during the past year—into three fairly distinct parts; the hunting man; the person who had spent ten weeks in Raymond Buildings; and the invisible being who shadowed the other two with his lordly ambition to produce original poetry. The sportsman was kicking his heels at home again with three much-loved horses that he couldn't afford to keep and no hope of hunting again with Norman Loder, who had now become joint-master of another famous pack—the Fitzwilliam—and was engaged to be married to an exceptionally charming girl who had been one of the boldest riders in the Atherstone country. Meanwhile the lonely occupant of those rooms in Gray's Inn had come away feeling that there was no particular reason why he should return to them again, since they had brought him nothing that appeared likely to lead him anywhere profitable. As for the invisible third, he, surely, was mainly responsible for the ineffectiveness of the whole affair. He seemed incapable of adopting a steady professional attitude to the problem of poetic production. He was undependable and desperately difficult to please. When asked 'What about your work?' he moodily replied that he must wait until he felt like it. He demanded unreasonable conditions of solitude and mental stimulation. He lost his temper, destroyed his manuscripts, and complained to the sportsman about never being allowed a fair chance to function because that impetuous individual associated himself with conventional people who didn't care a farthing about the arts. Thus—for four or five days—the actual Me who had the management of these ingredients sat worrying about them at Weirleigh, unable to see any way out of the dismal and irresolute situation to which he—and they—had reduced himself. He need not, however, have troubled; for the tragic turn of events which changed the world was about to take the trivial personal problem off his hands and set him on the road to unexpected success.

★ ★ ★

It will be remembered that until the last few days of July everyone was much agitated and concerned about the possibility of Civil War in Ireland, and the reports that things were looking rather black in the Balkans were less prominent in the newspapers than they deserved to be. My own awareness that trouble was brewing among the nations began the day after the Austrian ultimatum to Serbia, which was known on July 24th. This awareness was due to the arrival of a visitor—an old and intimate friend of ours—who had been a dashing Irish beauty in her youth, and was now the mother of two Colonels on the active list, both of them with records of distinguished service. The warm-hearted lady brought with her—as well she might—an atmosphere of undivulged War Office secrecies and a portentously head-shaking attitude toward the capitals of the European countries.

The presence of Mab Anley, with her well-founded forebodings, did much to accelerate and intensify my comprehension of the crisis as something which England couldn't keep out of if it ended in war; and the natural result was that I began—earlier than I might otherwise have done—to perturb myself about my own patriotic responsibilities. I offer this explanation because it has always seemed rather odd that I should have been so unwontedly quick off the mark as to have got myself medically examined for the Army by August 1st, and have been wearing my ill-fitting khaki on the first morning of the Great War. It must be added that this prompt acceptance of the inevitable was only achieved after a severe mental struggle—the climax of which will be described in the final pages of this chapter.

During those last days of July I still had a feeble hope that the whole thing might blow over and allow one to breathe freely again. But my heart was in my boots, like everyone else's, and a two-day match I played in for the Blue

Mantles did nothing to dispel the visceral sensation of approaching calamity. While the match was in progress several of the players were recalled to their naval and military stations. Nobody commented on their departure. We all knew what it meant. Early in the second afternoon the game ended in a joyless victory for the opposing team, and nothing was said about the next fixture on our card. Somewhat surprisingly, I had done quite a decent bit of defensive batting. For the first time in my life, however, I was unable to feel pleased about a modestly successful innings while on my way home. That evening I played *Prince Igor* with more expressiveness than ever, while Mrs. Anley sat on the sofa by the window, appreciative of my performance, but unable to conceal her opinion that God alone knew what we should all be doing in a month's time. My mother, whose courage was always unshakable, did her best to 'change the subject'; but she couldn't change the look in her own face.

Next day, which was July 31st, it seemed that any form of movement would be preferable to the intolerable suspense of waiting for further bad news. An article in *The Times*—in extra large print—had informed me that we should have to go to war in aid of France. A good long bike-ride, I decided—even if it didn't stop me thinking—

might perhaps enable me to think with a less benumbed brain.

Bicycling to Rye—a distance of thirty miles which I covered without dismounting—I felt very much as if I were pedalling away from my past life. My unseeing eyes were on the dusty road, and my brain was automatically revolving the same ideas over and over again. In the leisurely contentment of normal times I should have looked at the country and remembered how I had ridden over it with the Mid-Kent Stag Hounds. I should have stopped to note some place where I had jumped a fence into the road or a stile out of it. That sort of thing had now been wiped off the map. Germany, France, and Russia were all rumoured to be mobilizing. As for me, I was merely resorting to restless exertion while disentangling my mind from its reluctance to face the fact that the only thing left for me to do was to mobilize myself into the Army. I had rushed to the conclusion that war was a certainty, so what else could I do but try to have a gun in my hands when the Germans arrived, even if I didn't know how to fire it properly? Having achieved this decision, which seemed embarrassing rather than heroic, I approached Rye feeling more relieved than elated. My uncomfortable apprehensions were still there, but I had made up my mind, and felt perspiringly peaceful. Red roofed and church-crowned, the hill-top haven of Rye was rather like the brightly-lit background of a stage scene. Its happy associations with golfing holidays were for the time being obliterated. It was merely a place I'd arrived at, where—like the quiet villages I had passed on my way thither—everything looked just the same as usual.

I ate a big tea, lit my pipe, and stared seaward toward Winchelsea from the friendly terrace of an old inn on what had once been the city wall. Having renounced independence of action (joining the Army meant that, I assumed) I now felt immune from any sense of responsibility. I had bicycled far and fast, eased my bewildered brain by exercise, and consumed a couple of eggs, three large cups of tea, and a lot of bread-and-butter and jam. I should have been quite put out if someone had told me that there might not be a war after all, for the war had become so much my own affair that it was—temporarily and to the exclusion of all other considerations—merely me! It even occurred to me that—whatever else I might be in for—there was no more cause to worry about money. And I did not need to be reminded that—not many days ago—I had been faced by a deplorably unfertile future. I was clear of all that, anyhow.

I have said that while bicycling to Rye I more or less put the past behind me. On my homeward journey—solitary with my shadow between the dusty hedges of high summer—I was at any rate travelling toward something portentous. Acquiescent and unperplexed, I was in no hurry now. The thought of a European war had become too dumbfounding and incalculable for contemplation. I was, however, conscious of it through a sinking sensation in my middle when I got off to walk up the hills. Observing that bicyclist from to-day, I find it difficult to imagine and share his emptiness and immaturity of mind, so clueless, so inconsequent, and so unforeseeing. Confronted by that supreme crisis, he rides to meet it in virtual ignorance of its origins and antecedents. For like most of his generation he was taken unawares by that which realistic observation had long regarded as inevitable. Confused and uncomprehending, he has no precedent to guide and instruct him.

I had steadfastly, though vaguely, refused to believe that England would ever go to war with Germany. Not being in a position to reason about it, I felt no more indignation—now that the catastrophe was a seeming certainty—than I should have done if a doctor had told me that I'd contracted an incurable disease. I should have been no better off if I had known more about

European politics and commercial ambitions and such-like causes of the conflict. I was starting with a clean mental slate, uncomplicated by intellectual scruples. I had lived my way to almost twenty-eight in what now appears to have been an unquestioning confidence that the world had arrived at a meridian of unchangeableness. At the worst, I had thought, the warlike demonstrations of the Germans might cause us to adopt conscription, and I had got as far as gloomily discussing that prospect with Norman Loder. But on the whole I had felt as safe about the future as I did about 'the next world'—since the idea of 'being snuffed out' was too unpleasant for acceptance by my sensual apparatus. I had, indeed, sometimes wished that I were living in more stirring times. No one could have been more unaware that he was in for one of the most unrestful epochs in human history, and that the next twenty-five years would be a cemetery for the civilized delusions of the nineteenth century.

In the meantime the incredible event was upon me, and I—the solitary cyclist on that sunlit empty road, traversing the contented-looking landscape which had always behaved so permanently for me—was blankly resigned to the impossibility of bicycling away from this tidal wave which was overtaking all that I had hitherto considered secure. I was, moreover, pedalling dutifully toward it, almost as if the German cavalry had already landed on the Kentish coast —' I who know no more about soldiering than a centipede ', I thought, remembering that absurd uniform I used to wear when I was in the Rifle Volunteer Corps at Marlborough, with its blue-and-buff tunic that was too tight under the arms and the bandolier which I had more than once worn upside down when arriving on parade.

* * *

My energetic ride to Rye had been fairly easy going, for I went by the level though indirect road which was just inside the Kentish border until the last few miles. I was returning by a hillier way, which is in Sussex until one gets to Lamberhurst. From there onward the five-mile journey was so familiar that under ordinary conditions I should scarcely have been aware of my surroundings, for I knew them as well as I knew the nine-hole golf course in Squire Morland's park, which I had just passed without any sense of reminiscent emotion. But now that the heat of the day was over and my mind relaxed, I found myself observing those last miles with a heightened perception of what they meant to me.

The landscape wore no look of imminent doom; no thunderclouds were above the sky-line; the weather was perfect, and devoid of all atmosphere of fatefulness. But the aspect of things was within me, imbuing what I beheld with significances of impending disaster. Those two hop-kilns on the rising ground above the road—in the past there had never been anything noticeable about them. Now they seemed half-tragic in their homely simplicity. Standing away from their lengthened shadows, they were transfigured by the low-shot light of this heart-absorbing evening. In the reddening glow of the setting sun their kindly cowls were like sign-posts pointing toward the ominous continent of Europe. Those local kilns stood for England—for Kent, anyhow—rustically confronting whatever enemy might invade the freedom of the Hastings road. Indistinctly I imagined myself dodging about among the orchards and hop-fields, letting off my rifle at Germans charging across the fields below. Very vaguely visualized Germans they were, entirely unrelated to Schumann—or even Richard Strauss, whom I had politely applauded at Drury Lane a few weeks ago. And what exactly we should all be doing was equally undefined, since my notions of warfare had been mostly derived from drawings in old numbers of *The Illustrated London News*, when Russia was fighting Japan and the Turks were having battles with the Bulgarians. All that seemed so remote that there was no sense in the idea of such things happening in one's own country. It was rather like a recurrence of William the Conqueror, 1066, or the Wars of the Roses, utterly unreasonable in 1914. I assumed that harmless places like the farm I had just passed would be plundered and burnt down. For the moment I forgot all about artillery, though one of my best friends was in the Field Gunners, and I had already written to him, lugubriously asking his advice about how one enlisted in the cavalry.

Meanwhile I continued placidly along the Lamberhurst road, with the Bayham woods looking sombrely romantic on my left, while on my right was that fruitful landscape which receded so contentedly to its low green hills. Lit by departing day was the length and breadth of the Weald, and the message of those friendly miles was a single chord of emotion vibrating backward across the years to my earliest rememberings. Uplifted by this awareness, I knew that here was something deeply loved, something which the unmeasurable timelessness of childhood had made my own. I saw it as something worth losing, and saluted it with feelings of farewell. And when I came to Kipping's Cross, where I must turn off the main road for the last two miles homeward—when I came to that life-known glimpse of the Valley between the old apple trees at King's Toll farm (it was there—on a golden May afternoon five years before—that I had been drawn toward my heart's desire to win recognition as a poet, while I was driving home in the dog-cart after a cricket match) then my thoughts found assured utterance, and I said to myself that I was ready to meet whatever the war might ask of me.

The years of my youth were going down for ever in the weltering western gold, and the future would take me far from that sunset-embered horizon. Beyond the night was my new beginning. The Weald had been the world of my youngness, and while I gazed across it now I felt prepared to do what I could to defend it. And after all, dying for one's native land was believed to be the most glorious thing one could possibly do!